# ONE DEADLY SUMMER

Too mean to die. That was Kid Cobain. Nobody could kill him – he was way too fast. Money couldn't trap him, for the Kid made plenty hiring his gun. Be it lawmen, pretty women or bounty killers in packs, no one could so much as slow him down. How then could one simple rancher ever hope to put him in the ground? Straight shooter Joe Longley stuck to him like a shadow, trapping him into a lethal showdown. As they faced each other at the trail's end, all that remained was to kill or be killed.

# ONE DEADLY SUMMER

*by*

Matt James

**Dales Large Print Books**
Long Preston, North Yorkshire,
BD23 4ND, England.

British Library Cataloguing in Publication Data.

James, Matt
    One deadly summer.

    A catalogue record of this book is
    available from the British Library

    ISBN   1-84262-386-9 pbk

First published in Great Britain 2004 by Robert Hale Limited

Copyright © Matt James 2004

Cover illustration © Faba by arrangement with
Norma Editorial S.A.

The right of Matt James to be identified as the author of this
work has been asserted by him in accordance with the
Copyright, Designs and Patents Act, 1988

Published in Large Print 2005 by arrangement with
Robert Hale Limited

Dales Large Print is an imprint of Library Magna Books Ltd.

Printed and bound in Great Britain by
T.J. (International) Ltd., Cornwall, PL28 8RW

# CHAPTER 1

## KILLING TIME

The Kid whistled softly in the dry afternoon air. He could use a cigarette but decided it would have to wait. He didn't mind waiting, providing it was for something worthwhile – such as some hardcase with a gun closing in on a man stealthily with killing on his mind. Better even – a pair of hard-cases.

He had waited beneath a big old cotton-wood in deep brush for almost an hour with only his thoughts and his hidden horse for company. This was just a few miles outside the town where he'd left his bloody calling-card for all to see. There had been a whole bunch out hunting for him at the start of the manhunt, but he doubted if any of them but Crites and Buckland were really determined to run him to ground.

They were pros.

His top lip curled in a sneer and he listened to the sounds of heat crackling in the thickets. Just imagine his former henchmen sinking so low as to hire out to the Coot River Combine, the fancy name for the small-ranch, no-money nobodies of Midas County, when they knew damn well he, the Kid, was just winding up a contract with the Combine's bitter enemy, the Yellow Sky Ranch.

The Kid had been free to go, his designated duties completed, the day the boss of Yellow Sky came to him with an additional fat wad of cash, along with one last request for his killer to wind up the 'great job' he'd done. The final gun play that would hammer the very last nail into the Combine's coffin while earning the gunslick a nice piece of extra change.

Well, he'd obliged, the money was now riding on his hip and his fat mare. He'd been ready to lose his tail and head west, when he realized two 'old pards' were leading the pack.

To the gimlet eye of Kid Cobain this amounted to base treachery and would be treated as such.

But if enlisting a couple of over-the-hill gunners to go after him was the best the Combine could do, so the killer mused, then they must be even more desperate than he'd figured.

A man would laugh if it wasn't so damn

hot, or if he didn't have to keep real sharp.

The truth of it was, he mused as he decided to roll a cigarette anyway, that even if Crites and Buckland might be getting on a tad for gunpackers, a man couldn't afford to take them too lightly. They were on big money, had something to prove after last night, and most important of all they knew the Kid and certainly wouldn't make the error of underestimating him.

He lighted up and gusted smoke carelessly into the air above his head. He was being both ultra-cautious and reckless at the same moment. That was part of his make-up. Sometimes even he didn't know what he would do next, which was just one of the many things Kid Cobain found fascinating about himself.

A man just never got bored, being him.

A solitary eagle drifted overhead and he watched it slowly disappear off Logan Parsons' west range. To the north-east lay Judgment Pass, twenty miles distant. The broken blue line of the Pennebaker Hills was to the south, beyond them the vast triangle of the Black Sands Badlands which split the cattle country asunder like a mighty scar. And roughly midway across the base of the triangle, right on the broken-up borderline where the semi-arid lands began, the Kid's destination, Psalmsinger.

He could make the hideout by tomorrow night, providing he could rely on Buckland and Crites to trail him up here and thus enable him to settle their differences, quick and clean. Otherwise he'd have to go find the bastards on what felt like the hottest day of the summer.

He scowled, then chuckled and told himself he now didn't much care if he shot them into doll-rags or not. Either way, he'd end up covered in glory and riding free as a jaybird, on account that was the way he finished every job – the reason why anybody who wanted a gun job done right hired the Kid.

Nothing could stop him. Take last night, for instance...

The Kid entered Clint Creek in the deepest night, the moon riding the south-eastern sky like a galleon, the desert night-chill biting deep.

He rode past a homeless drunk propping up a lamp-post, the last defiant carouser in all this crummy, shut-down town.

'Hey, buddy, got a quarter for a shot?' he slurred, and the slim horseman just shook his head. The bum only saw the shaking head under the black hat, not the face. It was important that none should know that Kid Cobain had come very late to the town that was the headquarters of what was left of the Coot River Combine.

He glanced back. The man had fallen full length, his sorry hat lying upsidedown beside him.

A Combiner – he shouldn't wonder. Losers one and all. And tonight was Yellow Sky's night to win big.

Parsons had begun to feud as just another envious little man attacking the big, and had somehow wound up as Chairman of the Board. The Combine was plainly on its lasts legs, but Parsons was still rabble-rousing and raising hell, hence the presence of a slender man riding a fat brown mare through the town's hushed streets.

Cobain adjusted his bandanna fastidiously as the horse clop-hoofed past the feed and grain barn. He liked to dress for an event. Tonight he sported a five-bit calico shirt and candy-striped pants tucked into the straight-tops of fine leather boots hand-crafted for him by a bootmaker in Kansas City. These were practical footwear with pointed, two-inch high heels which enabled him to prop, pivot, spin or take off on any surface including gravel or slick grass.

Once he'd been strolling along a gloomy back alley in Denver at night when a man with a big grudge to settle appeared round a corner with a six-gun in either hand, blasting. Down went the Kid on his haunches, his high heels dug deep and he was well able to lunge violently aside as the lethal lead reached for him, landing on his slim back and firing between upswinging legs at his ambusher, ripping off seven bullets until it was not a man any longer but a butchered carcass without a face that lay sprawled in the dirt.

It was, he recalled, number seven. The tally had grown since. There were men in his trade who claimed they never kept count. They lied. You remembered every one. Kid Cobain remembered them with pleasure.

He moved steadily towards the gloom-shrouded central block, not knowing for sure where his man might be, but figured that, as a man of means used to the easy life, the hotel might be the likely place to look.

The brown mare was carrying him quietly towards the narrow little unpainted hotel squeezed in between saloon and drygoods store, when a light touch on the reins brought it a halt.

The Kid closed his eyes tightly for a long

moment, then opened them again. This was always a good trick to enhance your vision at night. It worked for him now when he realized that what he'd taken to be a motionless rifleman seated on the hotel steps, facing the other way, proved to be exactly that. A big man with a big rifle.

'Son of a gun!' he breathed almost admiringly. 'These poor varmints are taking themselves serious.'

He eased Maybell into an alley and stepped down, allowed the reins to drop. No need to tie this cayuse. He needed it to be ready to run at a moment's notice, which was often all the notice you got in this game.

A ghost in downy slippers would have made more noise than the gunslinger as he eased through the gloomy alleys that brought him out in the narrow space between saloon and hotel. The Cattleman's was only a six-roomer, but he couldn't go rattling door to door looking for a grizzled range-boss with a big nose and notions above his station in life.

He would have to check the register.

He tested the rear door. Locked. Figured.

Kid Cobain stood a moment in the chilly dark limbering up his friendliest grin before tracking up the side of the building to emerge up front not six feet from where the

11

burly man with the rifle was squatted on the edge of the porch.

'Howdy, pard,' he said amiably, stepping out into a patch of slanting moonlight. 'Happen to know if they got any vacancies in this here roach-trap tonight?'

The man was on his feet glaring at him over the rifle. He was startled and was sore that he'd shown it.

'What ... who ... where the hell did you come from?' he sputtered.

A picture of youthful ingenuousness, Cobain sauntered to the steps and rested a hand upon the rail. 'Chisum City,' he said, jerking a thumb. 'Heading for Panamint. Thought I might make her in one haul but me and my nag both petered out.'

He was mounting the steps, smile firmly in place.

'Didn't expect to find anyone about at this time.' He halted as the muzzle touched his chest, registered confusion. 'Why the big shooter? What's going on here?'

After a long moment the man began to lower his rifle uncertainly to take a keener look at this seemingly amiable nightcomer. Big mistake. Cobain's right hand blurred. A Smith & Wesson .44 jumped into his hand and whipped across the sentry's forehead, opening it to the bone. Strong despite his slender build, the gunman caught the falling body, dragged it into the shadows and let it slide limply to the boards.

He was inside in moments.

A dim light burned at the scarred desk and he was leafing through the buckram-bound ledger when sounds came from the hallway. Gun in hand, he whirled to confront a middle-aged man clutching a candle-holder in one hand and a revolver in the other, blinking at him.

'Thought I heard somethin'. Who be you? Did Hendry let you in...?'

It was his man.

The Kid's gun belched fire and smoke and the figure was hammered back into the hallway, both hands grabbing at his chest, going down with a great clatter of sound.

The noise barely reached the killer's ears as he streaked out through the open front door and vaulted the railing to cut left, limber legs eating up distance in six-feet strides. The plan had been to kill Parsons quietly and ghost out of town as he'd come, but the big man had literally jumped the gun on him. But he wouldn't be organizing any more mobs or bothering Burning Sky ever again.

The job was done, but noisily. Legs, do your stuff!

Lights were winking on and the speeding killer heard doors and windows screeching open as he swerved into the laneway on flying high heels. One bound took him into the saddle and he was on his way, bursting back into the street and leaning low over the mare's thick neck, steel spurs lightly raking horse hide.

Men poured into the street behind as he pounded between one of main street's three lights, his hat flapping by its thong, blond hair a banner.

'It's Cobain!' a hoarse voice shouted. 'He just killed Parsons! Stop him!'

Ahead now, two men brandishing six-guns. They looked familiar. Triggermen from the south, not young any more but still capable. Crites and Buckland really knew how to shoot.

With a vicious jerk on the reins he cut the mare for a side street's yawning maw, heard a Texan twang holler, 'It's the Kid for sure. Don't let him....'

The words were lost as the racing hoofbeats welled up against the buildings and drowned out all other sound.

He shot into the open travelling at a flat

gallop, and not even Crites and Buckland dared come after him by night. But they would come.

The images of false fronts soaring against the night sky and gunflashes in the darkness faded and the Kid realized the sound of a hoof striking stone was here, now, and close by beneath the old cottonwood tree.

He straightened sharply. The noise was a fair way off, and he was well-protected by the surrounding brush. Even so he was instantly on his feet and as intensely alert as though he hadn't spent a moment in reverie.

He knew if it proved to be anybody but his two, he would simply swing a leg over Maybell's back and mosey off. He'd done his job, had no grudge with whatever friends or citizens who might feel moved at least to put on a show of hunting for Parsons's killer. But Crites and Buckland – that was a cat of a different colour. They'd recognized him, knew where he hung his hat on odd occasions, which could pose an ongoing threat. But most tellingly, the killers had plainly signed on with the Combine knowing he was contracted to Yellow Sky.

That amounted to a double-cross no

matter how a man looked at it.

He was brushing dust from his striped pants when a voice called, 'We'd best check out the brush. I'll take left, you go right. We'll meet by the cottonwood.'

'Right. But I reckon he's got to be long gone by now, don't you?'

The reply was muffled, but Cobain whispered, 'You hope, Crites ... you broken-winded has-been!'

He waited with head cocked, tracking them by sound; Crites coming in from the north and Emil Buckland entering the brush warily on the western side.

Backing up from the tree, the gunman turned silkily and eased away south. The mare was tethered in a draw two hundred yards distant. She would make no sound, no matter what. Neither would he. By the time he'd put fifty yards between himself and the cottonwood he had both hunters to his north. He eased west a little then, deciding to deal with Buckland first.

'Hey, Buck boy!' an invisible Crites hissed loudly. 'You draggin' the chain over there?'

'Keep your shirt on.' Buckland's voice was thin and dry. He was scared, Cobain thought with contempt. He had every right to be.

Soon he was positioned in a draw directly below the animal pad Emil Buckland was following through the brush. He moved deliberately to stand in the open, guns housed, a smile puckering the corners of his mouth. Now, suddenly he could see the long, narrow face and bobbing shoulders of Buckland above his horse's head, man and animal both looking in the wrong direction.

Buckland held his six-gun in his right hand. The horse was sweating heavily. The gunfighter was in his mid-thirties and looked fifty. That was what the life could do to a man.

The Kid's contempt was boundless. Old, slow and riding for the wrong people, he sneered to himself.

Three strikes and you're out!

'Howdy there, Emil!' he called softly.

Buckland gasped as he reefed the horse to a halt and jerked around to find himself staring down at an empty-handed Kid Cobain, standing smiling in the full wash of afternoon sunlight. The rider's gun blurred upwards. It only had to rise another six inches to reach firing level. But the Kid was coming clear with both guns, drawing, aiming and triggering all in one blinding moment of incredible speed. Buckland's weapon tumbled from his hand and he stared stupidly at his bullet-shattered arm. He looked up imploringly but the next slug slammed him from the saddle to hit the ground like dead meat. He stared up in agony and feeble hope as the slender figure loomed over him.

'God's mercy, Kid – for old times' sake–'

'That's why I'm doing you a favour, Emil,' he said, and shot him between the eyes. 'For old times' sake.'

A horse was crashing through the brush as the Kid stood calmly reloading. He stared expressionlessly at the blood soaking the dry grass. 'Over here, Crites. No call to hasten. I'll be right here.'

Crites had always been a top-drawer gun, skilled and instinctive in a crisis. He feinted a pass on the left then jerked his mount right at the last moment to bring it racing along a tangent line east of the Kid's position.

As the Kid whirled smoothly to face the challenge, Buckland cut his mount broadside on then dropped down on the blind side to fire beneath the animal's neck with one boot hooked over the pommel, displaying all the supple skill of an Apache.

The slug whistled perilously close, forcing

Cobain to hurl himself to the ground, erasing his smirk. Instantly his guns bellowed and the bay horse was crashing down on to its knees, the rider kicking clear the split second before it somersaulted. Buckland was hurled violently against a stump and was plainly hurt as he struggled to his feet, ashen and bloody-faced, but still clutching his Colt.

Coming up off the ground, Cobain was disappointed how easy it was going to be, after all.

'Come on, Crites, you can do better than this. What happened to the big names you've put away that all your tenth-rate toadies are always bragging about? Are you just gonna whimper and bleat and have me put you down like an old hound dog whose time has come? Is that how it's got to be?'

Hector Crites had a shirtful of agony. Busted ribs and internal bleeding, he figured. He staggered, retched and groaned convincingly then suddenly snapped up straight to touch off a lightning shot that found its target. Cobain cursed. So the old dog had been foxing after all! But in the same instant he was triggering two-handed, mighty hammer blows knocking Crites flying, yet not putting him away. Not yet.

He wanted the man to grovel. It didn't pan

out that way. Crites was strong as he knelt in the dust and blanketing heat of this nameless hillside, ready to meet his Maker and telling it like it was.

'You are scum, Kid.' His voice was steady. 'At least they'll remember me as a pard who played it straight, but men'll spit whenever they drop your name for a thousand years because you were born a bloodless nothin', always been a nothin', will die a nothin'. I'll be waitin' in hell for you, you stinkin' little—'

Cobain's irons churned for the final time. For a moment he was stung, almost hurt. But only for a moment. He should care what an old gun bum thought of him?

He left them where they lay to go fetch his mount from the draw.

He pushed the mare west first, towards the stone country. The posse would chase him some, but not too far. He was leaking a little blood from a crease in the thigh, which meant he would take a long sweep round and stop by at Coyote Bluff.

They had a doctor at the Bluff. He hoped he wouldn't be too drunk.

## CHAPTER 2

## LONGLEY'S KINGDOM

Longley pushed the door of the wellhouse wide with the barrel of his Winchester, then stepped inside.

Nothing.

Just the stone-rimmed well, the bench, the winch. No uninvited visitors – such as scorpions, rattlesnakes, wandering Indians or gunhung drifters lurking here waiting to jump a man.

He grinned, even though he was not an easy-smiling man. The smile was part relief, part self deprecation. After all, the gunman who'd stopped by a couple of days back was about the closest to anything resembling trouble he'd ever seen here on six-section Tadpole Ranch, he reminded himself. Yet as he knelt on one knee to haul up the jug of cold milk the woman kept out here for him, he knew that if that hardcase should happen by here tomorrow he'd still be just as wary. Too late for caution after a man got jumped.

The milk was cold and sweet. He wiped his

mouth with the back of his hand, lowered the jug down into the darkness again by its rope then rose and went out, heeling the creaking door closed behind him.

The horse whiskered but the man paid no attention. Times like this towards the end of a hard day on the range, Joe Longley liked just to stand with his weight on one leg twisting a quirly and looking over his piece of land with an admiring eye, even though most folks would likely think it didn't look all that much.

The ranch house sat in a cluster of cottonwoods on a rise above Crooked Creek. Half the Tadpole was tolerably good grassland and meadow, the rest broken country, serried and gaunt looking. The caprock formed a cupped wall around the southern boundary, reaching all the way to Bill Haines' neighbouring BH Ranch.

A scatter of raw, weather-beaten buildings, a corral of round oak poles and a three-room cabin and barn comprised the headquarters. But it all looked just fine to him, sagging fences and unpainted planking notwithstanding. When he looked the Tadpole over like this, what he was really seeing was all the days, months and years spent scouting for the army, trail-bossing other men's herds north to the markets or hunting the big shaggies out on the buffalo plains, that it had taken to get his grubstake together, buy a piece of land and start in working for Joe Longley and nobody else.

He glanced towards the house and corrected himself mentally; well, for himself and the woman, he supposed.

Times when he was out on the back section or maybe off hunting game for the table, he could half forget he shared his life these days. But he always remembered real sharp when he returned to the home acres, wondered at moments like this how he'd ever thought he could just set up shop to hell and gone out here on the southern Kree Plains, with his nearest neighbour five miles away, and not slowly start dying of loneliness right off.

Marita had taken care of that, and he saw her appear in the doorway as he swung a leg over the dun and headed in.

She didn't wave. She wasn't demonstrative. He flicked his butt away and frowned. Maybe the same went for him. So he threw her a wave anyway. Her arms remained folded but he did see her smile. Faintly. She was a serious person, which, he supposed, made two of them.

A flight of ducks burst up from the pond

he'd dug into the south bank of the creek. They rose in noisy disarray then flattened out, flying in low formation across the east graze, skimming the coarse graze and quacking derisively at a bunch of cows.

The ducks were good judges, Longley mused. His cows were nothing to brag about, and were ungrateful to boot. The whole herd hadn't presented him with more than a score of calves this season, the hens had stopped laying – and yet the woman still couldn't understand why he was considering taking on a job away from Tadpole to boost their bank balance.

He wondered if she would raise the subject again at supper. Most likely. Women were like that, or so he was slowly coming to learn.

Longley offsaddled at the barn, watered the dun then washed up at the trough. He slewed water over his face and head, ran his fingers through his hair then exchanged menacing stares with the mule in the corral as he crossed the ranchyard.

He was a tall man of thirty, wide of shoulder and narrow of hip. He looked like a man who'd spent more time in the saddle than out of it. He had a slow, long-legged walk and didn't waste energy in anything he did. His sharply-etched, almost gaunt features were topped off by a thatch of thick dark hair that had to be kept trimmed or it ran wild. He wore faded dungarees and scuffed riding boots and a flat-brimmed brown hat. He climbed the three steps that led to the little porch, paused to remove his hat before going inside.

'Coffee?' she asked, not turning from the stove.

He grinned as he sat at the table. She was a cool one. Seemed nothing could flap her. She said the same thing about him. Maybe that was part of the secret whatever-it-was that had drawn them together from the day she first wandered in from the badlands, afoot, torn clothes, battered and bruised and barely able to walk.

He'd invited her to stay until she recovered – and that was over a year ago now. He'd never asked who she was or what had befallen her, and she didn't delve into his past which suited him fine, him being a private kind of man. They just seemed to suit one another and Joe Longley knew she cared for him, even though they really didn't talk about that either, just showed it, the way she did now when she came round behind him to place his steaming mug on the table then kissed the top of his head.

'*Hombre*,' she said in her husky voice. Then she sat opposite and clasped her hands, looking at him directly.

'So?'

'So?' He pretended not to understand.

'Do not play games with me, Joe. You said you would decide today. Have you?'

He tasted his joe. Delicious.

'I'm going to wait until they come again before making up my mind. If they come.'

She leaned back in her rickety chair, her face a smooth olive mask, eyes dark.

'They will come. They need you. The killer said that himself.'

'You don't know he's that, Rita.'

'Killer,' she reiterated, staring out the door. 'The guns, the walk – the way such ones talk and look at you as though they carry the power of life or death. At least let us agree on that point, Joe. Morell is a killer and we both know it.'

'You could be right.'

'I am. And I do not want you to have anything to do with such a man even if he seems to have money to burn.'

Longley simply nodded as he reached for his tobacco. That was just it. The broad-shouldered man with the tied-down six-shooter and the palest eyes he'd ever seen who'd stopped by the spread a few days back ago now, did have money. Lots of it. He'd hauled his roll from his pocket not once, but twice during their discussion. It was thick as a plank, and Morell had flipped it in the air once and caught it just to demonstrate how little big bucks meant to him.

They meant everything to Joe Longley, and Morell had smelt his need.

'Just think, Mr Longley ... you help track down these low-lifes what stole that hoss off my client ... doing just the sort of thing you've been doing on and off all your life so I'm told, and what do you get for your trouble? Two hundred? Chicken feed. How about five? Think of that, five hundred iron men just for finding a man's nag for him. Forget about it. Mr Vallance wants the best and everyone says that's you. So he's willing to pay the best to get the best. I'm here to tell you one thousand greenback dollars is the biggest payday you'll ever get to see if you live to be as old and broken down as this ranch house of yours. So, what do you say? And you, Mrs Longley, what–?'

'I am not Mrs Longley,' Marita had cut in sharply. 'But I say no. No horse is worth that much.'

'Champion is,' the gunman assured. 'Unchallenged winner of the Master Breeders Association's stud horse of the year award last year, sire of more racing champions than you could poke a stick at – and gone! Mr Longley – Joe, do you love horses? I mean, really love 'em?'

'I guess.'

'I can tell you you've never seen a horse like this. Maybe the finest thoroughbred sire ever seen in this country ... stolen, gone ... out there!'

At that point the pale-eyed man from the south had leapt from his chair to jab a finger north where the distance-hazed outline of ochre-coloured hills marked the southern sector of the Kree Plains and all the primitively magnificent stone and canyon country lying beyond.

'Joe, you owe it to yourself, to a fine citizen like Mr Vallance and to the goddamn United States of America to take this job on. Just give the nod and I'll hand you a two-hundred-dollars retainer on the spot. That's how good your reputation is. What do you say?'

What Longley had said was he'd think it over. They'd parted on that note, the gunman so confident of his eventual agreement

28

that he predicted Mr Vallance would most likely start off on his manhunt from Stud Horse Ranch and pick him up en route, just to save precious time.

Longley finished rolling his cigarette. He lit it and blew a cloud of smoke into the air. He watched it drift and couldn't help but notice the hole in the roof where the rain came in. It was not a big hole but it was there.

'Joe....'

He got up.

'I'm still thinking on it.'

'And I know you will reach the right decision.'

'Maybe.'

He was making for the door when she rose and said firmly, 'Whatever you decide, either to take the job or refuse it, I know it will be the right one.'

He looked down at her. She would be as good as her word, he knew. Whatever he decided. She was a mystery he would never attempt to solve – nor analyse his feelings for. He slipped his arm round her pliant waist and they were moving together out on to the porch when suddenly she stopped, smiled and drew away for the pantry.

'I just remembered,' she said. 'You know

how just this morning you said the corn was slow, there were fewer calves than we expected and the mule's temper was worse than ever?'

'I did all that griping?' he smiled. 'Just at breakfast?'

'I do not blame you.' She took something from a container and held it up before his face. It was an egg, smooth and brown. 'What is this?'

'An egg.'

She gave him a playful push. 'Not just an egg, Joe. Bidi's egg.'

It took a moment to remember she had names for all their chickens, a little longer to place Bidi, the speckled Rhode Island Red. His dark brows lifted. 'She's started laying again?'

'After six months. Is it not wonderful? You see things are never as difficult as they may seem.'

Out at the corral, feeding corn pellets to the mean-eyed mule through the oak railings, Longley was thinking that she must be right as he glanced around his empire. The sun was gone and in the soft light before the night wind brought the dust, the cornstalks seemed a healthier colour and the sound of a dogie calf blatting for its

30

mother sounded pretty cheerful, he must admit.

As though drawn by some force, his eyes swung due north. At this hour the distant Kree Plains were nothing more than an ochre-tinted haze on the far horizon, the hills beyond them barely visible with nothing at all to hint at the vast and mighty canyon country farther north.

But the man of the trails could see it all in his mind's eye as vividly as he'd done the last time he'd been up there, free and untrammelled, riding as scout for a bunch of wealthy southern hunters who slept in silk-lined tents every night.

The hills had been alive with game that season. Cottontails shot away for the closest cover at their approach. There were more deer than he'd ever seen, yet his brandy-tippling clients had been unable to bag even one, leaving it to him to bring down a doe for supper. Jackrabbits didn't bother diving for cover; they shot away through the open, relying on sheer speed for safety.

On one occasion they'd surprised a handsome grey wolf feasting on a kill. For a moment the startled animal seemed to be rushing towards the horsemen who screamed to the scout to finish it off. Longley could have killed it blindfold but missed with three shots, deliberately missing by a mile.

Halfway to the canyon country they'd caught up with a mob of wild turkeys which saddle-trotted ahead of the party for a mile and more before breaking off.

There were no turkey-gobblers up in the Burning Stone wilderness, only a wild and soaring magnificence of titanic canyons, impossibly slender monuments of rock reaching a thousand feet into the sky, shattered towers, ruined battlements and, dominating all else, the rearing, vermillion-tinted horizon line of ramparts formed by the mighty Barricades.

According to his gunman visitor, the thieves who'd stolen the rich man's prize horse were making for the Burning Stones – a great place to hide maybe, but no place to take a priceless and likely vulnerable stud stallion.

But what was all that to him?

With a burst of renewed energy he strode across to the two-acre cornfield and set about hoeing weeds out of the young corn. It was a bitch of a job by day with the sun slamming your back and sweat seeping out from under your hat, but in the cool of the evening it was a relaxing and easy thing to do where a man could work and think at the same time.

But after several minutes his work slowed and finally stopped altogether. He stood tall in the rustling cornfield, leaning on his hoe handle, gazing off towards the lights of the house.

She was that excited about one lousy egg!

He suddenly found himself trying to calculate just how many eggs could a man buy with $1,000. A million maybe? Two? And how many chickens, cows, acres, horses, pieces of farm equipment, tons of building lumber and pretty dresses for someone who deserved them?

He didn't raise the subject of the offer when she called him in to supper. But he sat down to table with a strong feeling under his belt buckle that if that horse rancher should stop by one day soon he just might have to think seriously about grabbing his offer. With both hands.

# CHAPTER 3

## MONEY FOR HATE

Robert Vallance had aged years in mere days. A tall and rugged man of almost fifty with the manner and look of someone accustomed to power and influence, he still carried himself with pride and arrogance, yet the violent incident which had virtually destroyed his fine valley horse stud several nights earlier had greyed his hairline and cut deep lines in his cheeks and round the eyes.

Yet still very much the man in control of his own destiny, Vallance was recovering and fighting back. His men knew it, his women knew it, as did the chairman of the Neverwinter National Banking Company.

The banker, who also happened to be Neverwinter's mayor, never called personally upon a client unless it happened to be the owner of Stud Ranch. The little fat man with the bullet eyes loathed the rare occasions he was 'invited' to make the ten-mile drive out to valley's premier horse ranch. Yet he always came. Vallance was that kind of client.

Standing in Champion's empty stall where the thieves had struck the previous Saturday night, Vallance showed no emotion as he stared out over the half-door watching the banker come waddling down from the house. His hands were locked behind his back and he rocked calmly to and fro on his heels, looking every inch the strong man he'd always been and certainly not a nervous customer about to demand a huge overdraft.

The reality was, that was precisely what he was today, and the banker paled visibly a short time later upon learning that one of his most valued customers required an immediate overdraft of twenty thousand dollars.

'T-twenty thousand, Mr Vallance? But ... but ... well of course I'm fully aware of your recent great loss and how it must affect you ... but twenty thousand? For what purpose, sir, might I enquire?'

'My estimated cost of recovering Champion,' Vallance replied evenly. Had he been truthful he might have correctly identified the purpose as 'recovery and revenge' but was too prudent for that. But having lost the sire which only last year had won the

'Supreme Stud Sire of the South-west' award by the Master Breeders Association, he insisted there was no option but to do all in his power to recover his marvellous meal ticket. A dying horse-thief shot during the midnight raid upon his stables had positively identified the rustler leader as the infamous Lucky Ned Chiller, Vallance informed; he'd also babbled over and over, something about 'the Burning Stone country', which in itself was enough to convince Vallance that he was in for a long and perilous pursuit. He insisted he would be successful, however. He'd already secured the services of several renowned and very expensive manhunters, he advised, some of whom the banker may have glimpsed up at the house already?

'You ... you mean those three on the gallery with the eyes like bank bandits and armed like the military?' the banker stammered. 'These are posse-men?'

'My kind of possemen.' Vallance was emphatic. 'More of the same kind will join us before I set out. I already have retained a top man to recruit and oversee the posse, and have been lucky enough to secure the most expert tracker and manhunter in the territory. Believe me, sir, I will recover my sire, return it to Stud Ranch and continue on exactly as before. As my personal banker you can rightly expect vast benefits to flow to the National, along with the swift retirement of my debt. Now, I'll send in an armed escort to collect the loan this time tomorrow. Does that fit in with your plans?'

'Mr Vallance, I can well understand your present state of mind. After all, I was there personally on the grand occasion when you won your magnificent award against all comers. I was especially gratified to be on hand to witness your triumph over your longtime rival in horse breeding from Utah – er, Petrie, wasn't it? Yes, Boss Petrie, a most arrogant and dislikable individual who–'

'Scum!'

The little man paled. 'I beg your pardon, Mr Vallance?'

The rancher's eyes were blazing. He seemed to twitch. But he quickly recovered his composure and forced an iron smile.

'Not you, Purtell. I was referring to Petrie, of course.' The smile vanished. 'Now, back to our business. Yes or no, I must have my answer immediately.'

Globules of sweat stood out on the banker's little fat face. He desperately wanted to request time to consider, to delay, hedge, perhaps even attempt to work up the nerve to say no. He did none of those things, less because Stud Ranch had always been a prized customer than the fact that Vallance had always scared him a little, today more than ever.

Even so, there was one matter he was obliged to raise, as any banker would: collateral.

Vallance's craggy features turned to stone. He'd known this had to come, but knowing didn't make it any more palatable. He objected, of course. It was mandatory. But both he and the banker knew he'd been running close to the edge with his line of credit recently, just as Robert Vallance well knew that, with his prize horse stolen, he had little of real value to offer as security but his ranch.

Purtell knew it also.

The banker now revealed he'd taken the liberty of having already drawn up an official bank application for the credit agreement listing not just part of Stud Ranch, but the entire spread, as the necessary security against the proposed loan.

Vallance was a hard man and a dangerous one, far more so than Purtell could ever

38

imagine. The raid on his ranch, and aspects of it which the banker was unaware of, had been a defining moment for the breeder. In anticipation of the bank's financing his venture, Vallance was already organizing a unique kind of manhunt which, if successful, would see him not only recover the stallion but see him avenge himself on an old and dangerous enemy.

Had the revenge component been absent Vallance may well have kicked Purtell clear off his land then set out to try and recover his Champion on a shoestring, even if certain such a venture was bound to fail.

He hid his feelings well as he nodded calmly in agreement. Of course Purtell would pay for his greed. But not yet. Compared with the man Vallance had in his sights, this usurious moneylender was miserably small fish.

The paperwork was completed in Vallance's front parlour with one of the rancher's 'possemen' seated framed in a window giving on to the gallery. The stranger was heavily built, dark eyed and olive skinned. He dressed in dark hues and sported a pencil-line black moustache and a revolver that appeared to have precious stones set in the base plate.

The last time the banker had seen someone like this he'd been trying to stick up his bank.

There was a trailhouse roughly halfway between Stud Ranch and Neverwinter. The banker never drank during working hours, but just knew, as his flunkey drove him from the ranch yard in his smart gig with the bright yellow wheels, that today he would simply have to stop off for a bottle at Big Charlie's, and quite likely finish it off before he got home.

He asked himself the same question a hundred times before getting there: how in the name of heaven could any kind of posse possibly cost a man $20,000?

Morell rode into the squalid cow-town in the dead of night long after the moon was gone, the stars just a faint haze across an inky sky.

He walked his tired horse past a woman standing on a corner. The last hopeful sister of sin smiled and made to speak but something held her silent. The rider was an impressive fellow with a V-shaped torso who sat his horse like a conquistador, yet even though he smiled down at her in the shadow of his hatbrim, showing strong white teeth, she still couldn't force herself to offer her weary proposition.

'Smart girl,' Morell whispered to himself as he passed on by. He tapped his nose with his forefinger. 'If a gal can't scent danger in your sweet trade she'll never get to make old bones.'

His smile vanished and he dropped a hand to gunbutt, simply for reassurance. This was regarded by those of his profession as a safe town to visit or set up a deal, yet simply because of the nature of that profession a man like him could never be really safe anyplace.

It was business that brought him to the river town tonight, and this killer was feeling edgy.

There were two reasons for this, the lesser being the huge amount of money involved in the proposed job. This client was offering big bucks all around, his own fee by far the biggest pay day he'd ever heard of, much less been offered.

This fact in itself was enough to cause even a true professional like Morell to act as cautious as a wily old hound in long-grass snake country. Yet the second factor was the element responsible for his edginess – namely the younger and by far the deadlier of the two men he was scheduled to meet with here tonight.

Nobody relaxed around that gunslinger kid he'd ridden fifty miles to meet, not even Morell.

He pushed on slowly towards the central square. He knew where he was to meet the rancher's contact man. The third man would meet up with both there – if he showed. With that one you could never be sure. He was half hoping the other wouldn't show, even if that might cost him his biggest pay day ever.

'The hell!' he muttered angrily, reining in sharply. 'You're starting to fuss like old Mother Grundy, Morell, damned if you ain't!'

Swiftly he swung down, looped the lines over his arm and began to walk.

He needed to unwind, he told himself. He must be ratcheted up way too tight even to consider missing out on this assignment, for any reason. No real man would ever back away from a job like this, so he reminded himself, not even if he did happen to hate the guts of someone else involved.

Morell had known from the outset he wouldn't be cast as top gun in this drama featuring rich men, a priceless horse and maybe more risks than he'd ever dreamed of, yet come curtain call this gunshark planned to be the one taking all the bows.

He smiled. He liked the theatrical analogy. Now where in hell was this dump's former Town Hall?

He finally found the decaying old ruin looming greyly above him on a side street off the square, hitched his horse in the alley close by and found his way back in the gloom afoot. After first testing the strength of the rickety old fire stairs he climbed athletically to reach the long, rectangular flat roof.

His right hand slapped gun handle as movement stirred over by the false front.

'Webb?' he hissed.

'Yeah. That you, Morell?'

'You better believe it.'

This was more like it, he thought cockily as he made his cat-footed way across to the tall figure. Once the game was in play and the juices began to flow, he always felt good, invincible even. Seven feet tall and fast as chain lightning with not a doubt in sight.

Webb was tall, lean, funereal and hard as nails. He ran Vallance's business affairs, hired and fired but held himself aloof from the breed of men he sometimes had to hire and fire. There were dead people in Webb's past, and even regular folks, although unaware of this fact, tended to keep their distance. So, isolated both from regular citizens and holding himself at arm's length from men like Morell, he lived a solitary life which suited him just fine. His very detachment helped make him a reliable judge of men.

Saddled with the task of organizing the biggest operation ever for rancher Vallance, Webb had immediately sought out a superior breed of gunslinger with both brains and a reputation as a leader and organizer, the qualifications that had first attracted his attention to the lithe-hipped man standing confidently before him now.

They didn't shake. This was strictly business. The business that had brought them together was horse-stealing, a crime that could get you hanged just about anyplace west of the Pecos.

Webb's employer was the famous breeder who'd recently had his top stallion stolen from under his nose by a gang of desperadoes who had thus far avoided every attempt to run them down.

Morell had heard all about the big steal before Webb contacted him, just at the time he'd wound up a risky assignment up north, for which he had been handsomely paid. The gunman had not been over-eager to work again so soon, but you never turned down a big-bucks client like the boss of Stud Ranch.

And yet Morell was both puzzled and a little wary as he stood on his windy rooftop with an unlit stogie clamped between his teeth. Sure, he'd just completed his first task for his new employer – making contact with a certain trail scout up on the southern fringe of the Kree. Yet it still didn't add up why a man like Vallance would be interested in doing business with him, a fast gun for hire with a crimson record. Even more mystifying was Webb's and Vallance's keen interest in yet another gunman of Morell's acquaintance, the other man he was to meet up with here tonight.

Didn't add up somehow.

But the money sure did.

'You get our scout?' Webb demanded in his brusque way.

'He's nibbling at the bait.'

'That's not good enough.'

'Who do you think you're talking to, you–' Morell flared, then bit his lip. The big one, he reminded himself. Don't screw it up. This was the man holding his ticket on the money train.

'I figure he'll ride with us,' he stated calmly. Then he added, 'Mr Webb.'

Webb glanced around impatiently. 'Where's your friend?'

'He'll show. But he sure ain't any friend.'

'He's late.'

'He likes to be late.'

'What makes you say that?'

'Look, Webb ... I mean, Mister. You're not doing business with horse breeders or bankers or folks who drink tea here, goddamnit. He's a gun, for God's sake. I'm a gun. We're different, we think different, act crazy half the time–'

'Speak for yourself, Lonely!'

Both whirled to see a slender silhouette appear from behind the battered canopy enclosing the interior staircase. Morell had his gun half out well before he'd identified the voice, shape and walk of Kid Cobain.

The Kid had startled him – the son of a bitch!

'It's OK, Lonely,' Cobain drawled, raising his hands and languidly dropping them as he crossed to them. 'I sorta got here early to eavesdrop just in case you shifty operators might be cooking up something sneaky. You know what I'm like.'

Morell bit his tongue, again. Cool and steady was the way to go.

'Webb, Cobain,' he introduced. He hooked thumbs in his shell belt and spread his shoulders wide. 'OK, listen sharp, Kid. Webb here works for the geezer who lost that stud horse and who wants to get it back more than you would believe. The law had already lost track of the thieves when Webb contacted me, and Vallance reckons he knows where the thieves went. He signed me on as ramrod and sent me north to line up the best scout big money can buy. At the same time he got me to make you an offer, then line you up to get checked out first. That's why we're here and that's about as much as I can tell you.'

The Kid made a languid gesture. 'Then I guess I know more than you already, Lonely.' He winked at the sombre Webb. 'He hates me calling him that, y'know. That's because he won't face facts. Morell's a big man with a gun, even bigger at setting up deals and mixing in big-money circles. But he's so sly and greedy and jealous of guys who are better than him with the Colts that he can't boast one friend in the trade. So, what else but Lonely, eh Lonely?'

'There's worse things to be than lonely,'

Morell replied pointedly.

Cobain turned to Webb. 'Who do you want killed?' He turned his head and winked sarcastically in Morell's direction. 'Funny thing, whenever they send for yours truly, it's always a killing job. You just know that's so, don't you, sober-sides?'

Webb stiffened but didn't bite. He was Robert Vallance's right-hand and a man of considerable influence. He was also a keen judge of character. He could smell danger coming off Kid Cobain stronger than the stink of rotgut whiskey.

'The man is right, Morell,' he said thinly. 'It's too late in the day to beat around the bushes.' He raked Cobain from head to toe with a gimlet eye. 'Well, I must say he looks the part, if a little scrawnier than I expected. And much younger ... just how old are you, Cobain?'

'Old enough to be the best,' came the soft reply. 'You can sign off on that, can't you, Morell? I mean, you're some big guntipper, sure 'nuff, but even you'd sooner eat red pepper than tangle with the Kid. Ain't that the simple truth?'

The man was trying to stir him, Morell knew. He wouldn't succeed. Not this time around the traps.

He said, 'Let's get down to cases, Mr Webb. How much are you offering the Kid, and what does Vallance expect him to do to earn it?'

'Mr Vallance is in deep shock,' Webb lamented. 'Stud Ranch has been victim of thieves several times in the past, and we believe the renegade who executed this last raid that saw us lose Champion has robbed us before—'

'He's talking about Lucky Ned,' Morell supplied.

'Ned Chiller?' The Kid sounded almost impressed. He laughed. 'Whooeee! That old Ned is a mean son of a gun, and I say meaannn! But maybe I'm catching on now. You want me along on your horse hunt as protection so bad old Ned won't get to bury you all? That about how it is, Webb?'

'You're thinking along the right lines but you don't go half far enough.'

Webb paused to raise himself to his full height. His long-boned face was pale and gaunt in the half-light, but his eyes held a deadly glitter.

'We're hiring this trailsman Longley who apparently has the intimate knowledge of the wilderness necessary to assist us run these vermin down no matter how far they might run ... and we have some notions on that factor also. And certainly we expect you gentlemen, along with others I have already hired, to protect us and see that we retrieve Champion in prime health and condition. But–'

'Hey, this better be a good "but" Loner,' Cobain cracked. 'We ask a question and we get a lecture–'

'Shut up, will you!'

The Kid blinked. Had Webb really spoken to him that way?

'Easy,' Morell said hastily, shooting Webb a warning look. 'C'mon, man, just tell us what we want to know.'

Webb tugged down the lapels of his dark seaman's jacket. His eye held a clear, cold glitter.

'The reason we are prepared to pay more money than you've ever seen, Cobain, is simple. You're not being hired as posseman or anything remotely like.' He made a gesture embracing both men. 'When we catch up with Chiller we intend to destroy him and every man associated with this evil deed. Do I make myself clear? There are to be no apprehendings, no survivors, just corpses. That is why I'm standing here talking with men like you two.'

Morell's jaw sagged. He stared blankly. Even the Kid appeared momentarily startled. Webb really knew how to make himself understood, in spades! Word was that the Chiller pack ran to some seven or eight men, so Webb wasn't proposing just a kill or two at trail's end of the big hunt. The man was talking wholesale slaughter!

The Kid's chuckle was a hot knife that finally slashed the sudden silence.

'Well, don't this beat all, Lonely? Last I heard, some bigwig was talking about making Vallance governor, he stands so tall. Now we find out the bastard's even badder than you and me, damned if he ain't.'

He held up a silencing hand and turned deadly serious in an instant as Webb made to interject.

'All right, what's your real game, Undertaker?' he hissed. 'You brought me fifty miles just so you can shovel me a load of bullshit? Money jokers might hire a gun to take out one mark or maybe two at most, but nobody lines up a whole bunch for the slaughterman, just like that. Which means this is some kind of con. Didn't anyone warn you I can't be conned ... and I sure as hell ain't got no sense of humour?'

'Amen to that,' Morell put in drily.

Webb was unfazed. 'Five grand,' he rapped. The Kid blinked. 'Huh?'

'Five grand if you get to take out Chiller himself, along with any two of his bunch,' the man affirmed. 'You can earn one thousand apiece for any others we might want planted as well.'

So saying he reached into a hip pocket to produce a sleek billfold, snapped it open. It was packed with large denomination bills. He fingered out a hundred dollars and sniffed it. 'It's true what they say. Blood money smells the same as any other kind. One thousand dollars down payment, now.' His eyes glittered in the deep gloom as a stray wind flapped his jacket. 'In or out, gunman? I don't have all night.'

Neither did the Kid.

He snatched the bill and snapped his fingers for the balance, smirking sideways at Morell.

'What'd I always say, Lonely? That one day I'd be the biggest ever, right? Looks like that day's come, eh, small-timer?'

Cobain was rubbing his nose in it. But Morell remained strong and silent. Suddenly his major job had expanded bloatedly to become the biggest ever, the one he'd been quietly preparing himself for all his life. In an instant his resolve became diamond hard, unchangeable. He would be rich by the time this horse-hunt was over, which almost certainly meant he would also have to kill the Kid. He knew he could do it. He and Sam Colt made a pairing that had never run second.

Joe Longley got out of bed each morning around five o'clock. It was a lifetime habit. Besides, the early part of the day was the time he liked best – that hushed, cool time before sunrise.

Today was no different from the day and days before. He rose quietly so as not to awaken the woman, gathered up his clothes and went through to dress in the kitchen. Then he washed and shaved and set the coffee on the stove before going out on to the porch.

He stretched and felt the ache in his shoulders from yesterday's work. A heifer had got stuck in the mud hole out by the sump and he'd had to muscle her out on his own rather than risk hauling her out with the mule.

He smiled faintly. He liked working with his hands, always had done. It beat daydreaming and buffalo dust hollow, that was for sure.

He frowned as he went back inside. He knew he was thinking about Morell and his offer now. He supposed he should have had more horse sense than give the gunman's proposal brain room for more than a few seconds, he reproved himself as he poured it hot and black. That sort of big-talking, big-bucks caper never comes to anything, Joe boy. You should know that. Three days now, and nothing. Marita was right. She hadn't liked Morell's style from the jump.

He took her in a cup in case she was awake. She wasn't. He smiled as he set the coffee down on the crate that served as a table. The woman lay with her hair dark against the pillow and her brown arms and legs long and beautiful, sleeping peacefully.

He took his joe out to the barn, the mule greeting him with a baleful bray from the corral. That critter expected to be fed every hour on the hour. Longley hated this animal that he'd had to settle for instead of acquiring himself a real mule with a head less resembling a chunk of black granite.

He ignored all the braying and kicking and went about his chores, feeding the chickens, two laying now, then his saddle horse – at least that was quality. He next took time out to run some fencing wire round Marita's cracked clothes-prop before heading off acro?? the yard again to check on the heifer.

His horse snorted.

He propped and turned sharply. The dun stood staring due south. Longley shaded his eyes with one hand. At first he saw nothing. Then the wind gusted and he caught a glimpse of lifting dust against the dark of the cedar line some two miles south. Narrowing his gaze he focused intently until able to make out the bobbing silhouettes of riders heading his way, one, two ... a whole bunch of men on horseback by the looks with some kind of wagon jolting along in back.

He whirled and strode back for the house, slowing when he saw the woman standing at the top of the steps holding his Winchester.

He shook his head. He still hadn't adjusted to the fact that Marita often seemed to anticipate his needs even before he was clear about them himself.

'Better get inside,' he suggested, relieving her of the rifle. 'Could be trouble....'

A glance passed between them. She never spoke of her past but he sensed it had been no bed of roses. There wasn't much to worry about out here, with one neighbour just a couple of miles away and a dozen more within ten. But the odd band of wandering Mescaleros wasn't unknown, while badmen and drifters sometimes came hazing south out of the wilderness with either trouble or the law on their tail.

The woman folded her arms and shook her head. 'That man with the gun who came here.' She sounded serious as she mostly was. 'What will you tell him?'

He looked away. He didn't know the answer to that yet. All he knew was just how much money was involved. He'd never been money-conscious until he quit the trails and settled down in one place ... and he knew that big-money offers to take on work of a kind that was second nature to him didn't come every day.

He knew that the Tadpole needed some cash money bled into pretty smart if they didn't want to start cutting corners even sharper.

He also knew that he didn't want to go against her, but would make up his own mind in the end. Like always.

Soon the riders could be defined as individuals and not just a dust-shrouded mass. Longley started in counting to reach eight or nine. He reached up and massaged the back of his neck. Even at this distance he could detect the glint of light on gunmetal, lots of gunmetal. Understandable they should come well-armed, he supposed. The gang they claimed stole the prize horse was said to be sizeable with a real mean reputation.

Lucky Ned Chiller.

He rolled the name round his tongue. Of course he'd heard of the Chiller gang before but always had the impression they'd made their name robbing banks and raiding gold shipments. Lifting horses, even top-of-the-range stuff like this Champion was reputed to be, didn't sound the sort of job that would appeal to hellions of that breed. It stood to reason that if you stole an expensive animal, you'd then have to sell it. That could prove a hard thing to do, for Vallance's stallion was famous and the whole territory would know who it had been stolen by.

He shrugged. Luckily he didn't know too much about how outlaws operated, even though he'd helped hunt down a few in his day.

Absently he massaged a deep crease in his left shoulder, the legacy of a posse he'd scouted trail for some years back. There had been seven possemen after just one mine bandit, yet the outlaw had killed two and wounded three, including him, before he was brought down. He supposed if he thought about what he knew of this current situation honestly, he'd have to assess Chiller as the breed who might take a lot of men with him if he ever got cornered.

It was thirty minutes before he could positively identify Morell amongst the horsemen. With a nod he set the Winchester aside and put in another quarter-hour churning butter before Morell led the party splashing across the creek and they came up the slope at the canter.

Longley nodded a greeting as they approached. There was no chance of mistaking Vallance. The horse rancher was a big broad fellow radiating outdoor authority that you sensed even before he'd opened his mouth.

The posse was worth a second look, then another. Longley had anticipated ranch hands and trailsmen, but apart from one or two obvious wranglers the party comprised a trio of dangerous-looking gunpackers sporting heavy hardware and stony faces. They studied him through narrowed eyes and seemed to take in everything about him and his place at first glance.

They were the Morell type, he figured. Likely better with guns than with horses. But maybe that was the breed you wanted with you when you set out to run down an outfit like the Chiller bunch.

Morell appeared self-assured and confident as he swung down to perform a perfunctory introduction: 'This is Mr Vallance, the tall feller is Webb, his right-hand man, the rest you'll get to know on the trail.' He rested hands on hips, a characteristic gesture. 'Well, pard, you ready to ride?'

Longley heard but didn't respond immediately. In back of the riders, most of whom were swinging down to stretch and spit, and beyond the sturdy covered wagon, he glimpsed a lean-bodied youngster sporting a blood-red shirt and flash boots with embroidered stars. His hat was tilted low over his sharp-featured face and he appeared intent on staying in the background. Yet he seemed to attract attention without effort, while the fact that he sported twin revolvers slung low on lean hips didn't go unnoticed.

Longley turned his head to see the woman watching from the porch. Her gaze was also focused on the youth at the rear, that's if he was a youth.

'Who's that?' he asked Morell, jerking a thumb.

The man turned to look. 'Oh, him. That's just the Kid. Now, as I was saying–'

'This seems a mighty strange kind of posse you've saddled up here, mister.'

'You can believe that, trail scout,' Vallance chimed in, peeling off his riding gloves. 'But not half as strange as the simple fact that you are looking at a man who is facing ruin if he doesn't recover the finest animal in the country ... and would hire the devil himself if he decided that would help see him achieve that result. Now, I'm dry, I'm in a hurry and I want to talk to you in private.' He gestured at the house with his hat. 'Care to show us the way?'

For a moment Longley appeared about to baulk, to teeter on the verge of changing his mind and calling it all off there and then. But he didn't. He had one thousand reasons for not doing so.

He jerked his chin and Vallance, Webb and Morell followed him across to the house.

# CHAPTER 4

## DEVIL BIRDS, DEVIL'S MARBLES

The posse drummed through the ghost town of Yegua around two in the morning in the deep darkness after moonset and before the first hint of dawn.

The ghoster boasted but a single occupant, a half-crazed old sourdough who'd lived there alone for a decade ever since the veins played out. Mostly he was left alone from one year's end to another, for Yegua was isolated, ugly, spider-haunted and perennially short of water. Yet blinking out at the dark column of silent horsemen clattering past the thirty-room hotel he now had all to himself, he shook his grizzled head and wondered if this mightn't be a sign for him to move on. He couldn't take all this activity. He'd seen not a single human being over the past twenty months, yet this was the second time a heavily armed party of dangerous-looking horsemen had invaded his solitude just this week. A man could only take so much overcrowding.

Longley didn't know about the other party taking this route; none of them did. The restless winds of the Kree Plains this time of year erased most traces of man's passage within a matter of hours.

He'd led the party along this almost-invisible old wagon route flanking the plains on the eastern side simply because it offered the quickest route – if toughest – across the east Krees if your destination happened to be the Burning Stone wilderness, and Vallance insisted that was where their quarry was headed.

How the big man knew, guessed or calculated this his trail scout was yet to learn.

Longley hipped around in the saddle to check on the bobbing heads of men and horses, double checking that they were still all together.

He counted nine which included Vallance and Webb, night-travelling in the rugged four-wheeled covered wagon, and the driver. It was the correct tally. They hadn't hired him to concern himself about stragglers or drop-outs, it was simply instinctive. When you hired Joe Longley as trail boss of your outfit then you got the whole thing, for that was the only way he knew.

The horses began to labour when they hit the steep rise beyond the town. A huge rusted gantry which had once dominated the biggest of the ghoster's six copper mines suddenly loomed from the darkness then quickly fell away behind.

Longley looked over his shoulder to watch the edifice vanish and continued to stare back into the maw of the night, beyond Yegua and the plains, envisioning all the long horse-miles back to the Tadpole.

She hadn't wept but he knew she'd wanted to. Neighbour Haines and one of his husky sons had offered to help out, and Longley had provisioned up the larder ahead of time, sensing even before meeting up with Vallance that he was going to take this job.

He'd been surprised by her distress. He'd always thought of her as tough and tolerably unemotional, like himself. They lived like lovers but never mentioned love. He didn't miss her; that would be loco. Yet out here in the big dark of the plains night he had to concede he'd feel better if she was riding along with him – and his mighty strange outfit.

The more he saw of the rich man's posse, the less like a posse it seemed than any he'd ever had anything to do with.

Clancy, the laconic buggy-driver and cook from Stud Ranch, seemed about the only regular joe in the whole bunch.

Vallance himself acted like a man on a life-or-death mission. The man seemed driven and obsessive and up until this point in the hunt had kept mainly to his rig with Webb and the driver, leaving Morell and Longley to select the trail and maintain the hunt for sign.

Webb, whom Cobain had dubbed 'the Undertaker', resembled a hanging judge or a hard-sell preacherman with contempt for everyone who didn't see eye-to-eye with his hard-line theology.

There were varying shades and sides to the Stud Ranch trio, but with the three gunpackers whom Vallance openly referred to as his 'mercenaries', what you saw was plainly what you got.

Dalton was a solid, steel-eyed Kentuckian who dressed expensively in broadcloth and had a lot of style, for a shootist.

Flashy Flagg was a highly strung, almost jittery two-gunner from Denver who fancied himself with the ladies and carved notches on the showy brass-and-mahogany handles of his twin Peacemakers.

Santone was the strong man from the

south and natural leader of the gunmen, a black-moustached man of around forty, mixed blood, with a sleepy-eyed look that concealed a rare talent for violence that had seen him survive long in a profession where men died young.

Then there was the Kid.

There was something about Cobain that set a man's teeth on edge, and even a widely travelled Longley had never struck anyone quite like him.

That he was about as dangerous as they came was something you sensed right off, before you listened to any of the stories about him. He was strictly a loner who seemed fascinated by his own company and the uniqueness of being Kid Cobain – killer.

He boasted about his kills, and men like Dalton and Flagg could confirm his stories if a man was interested enough to ask.

Longley wasn't. He was trail-bossing this outfit and his job was to take the man who hired him wherever he wanted to go, and make sure they didn't get ambushed or run out of water, and eventually caught up with the Chiller gang – whenever the hell that might be.

But why this route? Why north?

He focused once again on the way ahead.

Emerging in the grey light of early morning sprawled the vast monotony of the desert plain, studded with mesquite and prickly-pear cactus, reaching out towards the criss-crossing arroyo territory which divided the Kree Plains on their east from the hard-scrabble cattle lands far to the west.

He asked himself for the hundredth time: how did the rancher know the Burning Sky was the rustlers' destination? Or was he just guessing?

He shook his head.

Were he a horse-thief with a priceless stolen stallion to get rid of, the last compass point he would consider was north. To the east, west and particularly in the verdant south of the undulating grass plains of which Stud Ranch comprised about five thousand prime acres, were scattered pueblos, hamlets, towns and even a city or two. You had a railroad, several big rivers, markets, thieves' kitchens, even remote and hidden green backwaters where a good thief could hole up with his horse for a time while things cooled down before heading off to trade it off for big dollars.

Up here there was a handful of cobweb-haunted ghosters, just one medium-sized town around halfway to the border from here, then nothing but hundreds of square miles of some of the most spectacularly beautiful and forbidding territory in the entire south-west.

If Vallance was so sure his gang of thieves were making for Utah Territory, just what the hell sort of shape did he expect his finely bred wonder-horse to be in by the time it had slogged its way across every canyon, basin, gulch, arroyo, ridge, bluff, range, escarpment, valley and rock hole of the Burning Stone Wilderness?

The miles and hours spun by and he was no closer to an answer. The whole affair just plain didn't make sense.

Finally he reminded himself of what he was being paid, which meant none of those concerns was his. He was responsible only for their safety, staying on course and keeping a sharp lookout for sign of their quarry, something both Vallance and Morell insisted they were sure to come across at any moment, or so they claimed.

He called a halt upon reaching a wooded basin where gnarled old cedars grew in numbers, their dense, fine, light-green foliage casting shadows inviting to the weary traveller. Longley had once rescued a bunch of westbound migrants who'd lost their way and had eventually fallen foul of the Mescaleros. He could have related a few hair-raising tales about that forty-eight hours of red hell, but sensed somehow this company mightn't be all that interested or impressed.

'Dalton,' he called as he checked out the horses. 'Tighten up your cinch or you're going to have a sore-backed horse by tonight.'

The gunman grunted and did as ordered, and climbing down from his buggy, a weary Vallance nodded approvingly.

In the background, seated on a patch of grass which he kept plucking and feeding to his fat mare, Kid Cobain chuckled to himself as if at some secret joke then leaned back with his hands behind his head and smiled up through the fluttering leaves at the sky.

They watered and grain-fed their mounts on Longley's instructions. The party ate and drank sparingly and the journey resumed at a mile-eating lope that carried them up from the basin to glimpse the pale wash of the false dawn far off to the east.

The heat built up rapidly as they fell back into the monotony of the plains. Riding lead, where he was in best position to pick up any sign before it could be blotted out,

Longley rode relaxed and easy in the saddle watching for landmarks he reckoned would be familiar only to him.

On the horizon's edge to the east, as they topped out a high point in the trail, the harsh sunlight struck something immensely tall and skinny-looking that resembled a giant's needle thrusting into the sky, but which was in fact the towering butte which had served as a vital landmark for the missionary Velez de Escalante seeking out the Old Spanish Trail during his historic pilgrimage north in 1776.

He was looking for another feature further north when Morell came up alongside on his paint pony looking fit and relaxed, as usual. 'You're doing good, Joe.' The man fingered his hat back off his head to let it hang on his shoulders by the throat strap. He winked. 'At covering a lot of ground, anyway. Sighted anything yet?'

'Let's say I've seen just about what I expected to see. Namely, nothing.'

'Still no faith, huh?'

He shrugged. 'I've got faith in the US dollar.'

'Nothing else?'

Longley pointedly glanced back over his shoulder. 'Nothing or nobody I see right now, leastways.'

'Still suspicious about this whole caper?'

Longley just shrugged.

'I'm getting paid. That's all that matters.'

'Funny thing about that, trail boss. You and money, that is. When folks kept telling me you were the man we needed for this job, they all seemed to think you couldn't be bought. But, hell, you just snapped it up. The *dinero*, that is.'

Joe studied the way ahead. He couldn't deny it. Once money had meant little; now it was all important. So? A man grew older and wiser – he hoped.

He pointed ahead to where a jagged row of peaks fanged the hot blue sky.

'Sawteeth Range,' he said. 'Beyond that line is the wilderness, yet we've still cut no sign. You sure Vallance wants us to keep on?'

'Dead sure.'

'Uh huh. Well, as you can likely see, the Sawteeth run horizon to horizon west to east. There's just three ways through for horses, and they're all tolerably close together. Seems to me if I was a thief, and had people dogging me this far, I might think about stopping them at those passes on account you'd never get a better opportunity.'

Morell sobered. 'Want to talk about this to

70

the boss?'

'I reckon.'

Vallance heard Longley out, took a long look at the distant range through his field glasses, and finally nodded.

'All right, scout, what you're saying seems to make sense.' He stroked his jaw. 'Just three ways through, you say?'

'The Slot about ten miles west, Squaw Pass roughly dead ahead, the Tunnel a fair ways off to the northeast, north of Crow Creek – that's the town and trading post I told you about,' Longley said. 'If you're asking me, I reckon we ought to make camp up ahead at Skull Spring then send Santone, Dalton and Flagg out to check out a pass apiece to save time.'

'Sound all right to you?' Vallance asked Morell, and the gunman nodded. 'Very well, see to it.' As Morell strode off, the big man nodded to Longley. 'How long do you estimate it should take them to get there and back?'

'Couple of hours each way plus, say an hour. Around five hours. Providing they don't run into your horse rustlers laying in wait, that is. If that happened I reckon you should tell them to go round up their pards before they try anything, or better still, come back and get the rest of us.'

'I'm paying big money to men who make their living with their guns, mister. If they should flush any Chiller scum lurking around those passes they can start right in earning that money. *Comprende?*'

'You're the boss.'

'But you still think I'm a little crazy, don't you?'

Longley was considering his reply when a swift stutter of hoofs brought the Kid across to them. He reefed back hard on the reins and spat in the dirt as the horse slid to a stop.

'What's the big idea, Farmer?' he snapped. He jerked a thumb. 'What's so special about them bindle stiffs?'

'What?' Longley replied.

'Picking them and leaving me out of it. Just on account they suck up to you and I don't.'

'Steady, steady,' Vallance placated. 'Why are you acting so sore, Kid? I gather you're saying Morell didn't pick you. If that's the case, isn't it your good luck.' The big man frowned. 'Unless you're saying you want to ride out there and maybe get shot at. Are you?'

'Well, if I see one lousy chance of doing

something other than clop-hoofing across a million miles of nothing with the most boring bunch of bastards I've ever struck in my mortal, then yeah, I want to go. More than that, Mr Boss-man, I am going. Ain't that so, Longley?'

Joe studied the Kid. His eyes were over-bright and he looked ready to take this all the way even though it was something of little importance. He looked a question at the rancher, who nodded.

'I don't give a damn,' Longley said then. 'I guess I didn't reckon you'd be interested.'

The Kid leaned from his saddle and rested his elbow on his thigh.

'That ain't the reason, sodbuster. You hate my guts. I saw it the moment I rode on to your miserable piece of dirt. You're one of them righteous, stiff-necked nobodies who shy away from guys like me like you're scared of catching something – or mebbe stoppin' six in the guts. Well, that's just fine by me, only you get one thing straight. We might have a long way to go together yet, who knows? But while it lasts, don't you mess with me or we'll be looking for a new scout. Get the notion?'

'Now, Kid–' Vallance began, but the other cut him off.

'I'm taking the Slot,' he rapped, hauling the mare back on its haunches. 'Around ten miles west of the dead-ahead point in those hills – that right?'

Longley nodded and the man heeled away, his back rigid with tension, and yet now he was whistling.

The two men traded glances.

'Has some growing up to do, that one,' was Vallance's comment.

'Maybe. Maybe he'll never make it.' Joe frowned. 'You know, I still don't understand why–'

'I know what you're going to say, Joe. But just be patient a little longer. Sooner or later I'll have to explain everything to you, such as how I know my Champion is up here somewhere and why I went out of my way to sign on men like Cobain and Santone. You'll understand everything then. In the meantime, just keep on the way you're going. You're doing a fine job.'

Longley just nodded and walked off to see to his horse. Across at the remuda he saw the Kid sling a water canteen over one shoulder, snarl something at Morell then take off north at the gallop, raising a billowing cloud of yellow dust.

'Hey, Miguel!'

'*Si?*'

'You asleep up there?'

'No, I watch the pass. What you do down there, *amigo?*'

'Keepin' sharp, of course. What do you think?'

'Is too hot to think... I think.'

The sons of a Kansas cattle-thief and a Mexican renegade occupied hidden lookout positions some thirty yards apart in the nest of granitic devil's marble which loomed directly opposite the dark gash in the Sawteeth foothills known as the Slot.

The jaws of the narrow pass yawned just as empty and lifeless in the late afternoon as had been the case throughout every hour of the day and a half they'd already spent here with their rifles, field glasses, a bottle of Metaxa and the unexpected one hundred dollars apiece they'd been paid for what was turning out to be about their easiest job ever.

'Just watch that pass and if anybody who even looks like trouble should show up, blast 'em to hell then catch us up at Prophet's Well and I'll pay you both a bonus.'

So offered the wild outlaw known as Lucky Ned upon showing up at Crow Creek looking to hire gunmen to stand watch out at the passes, upon meeting up with Miguel and Cody, a pair of hardcases down on their uppers and cadging drinks at the Chaparral House Saloon while watching out for someone to rob.

Thoroughly bored with his job by this, Cody was half dozing in his nest in the marbles but the Mexican was doing a conscientious job up above, sprawled out as motionless as a basking snake in a patch of rock shade with a battered set of field glasses fixed to his eyes.

Too good a job, as it turned out.

They heard nothing to alert them. This was due to the fact that the man approaching from the back of the rock formation had left his mount a mile back in a grassy draw and was now moving in as swift and quiet as a greased snake quitting a Sunday school picnic.

It was a quiet and drowsy ten minutes later when Miguel began to feel the eyestrain. He lowered the glasses to the stone between his elbows, pressed finger and thumb to the corners of his eyes, opened them, blinked, and lost his breath.

'Howdo, greaser. Thought you'd gone and nodded off on me there for a moment.'

The grinning man had appeared out of

nowhere to stand lazily across thirty feet of curved stone with one hand resting against the huge shade rock, the other on his hip above the handle of a Smith & Wesson .44.

The Mexican's mouth was dry as gunpowder as he began reaching for his rifle. He'd never seen the stranger before but knew at first glance that he was the worst kind of trouble. The eyes, the guns, the mocking smile said it all. He might have shouted a warning to Cody if his throat was not constricting so cruelly. His hands were on the stock of the rifle now and still the man made no move to draw, just went on leaning and smiling like someone really enjoying himself.

'Want to know where you slipped up, Mex?'

Now Miguel had both hands on his rifle – his shaking hands.

'Seems you were laying there so quiet for so long that those rascals just had to come check you out in case you were dead.'

The Mexican raised his eyes to glimpse a pair of Sonoran buzzards planing away eastward, and tears of chagrin filled his eyes. Devil birds! He'd always hated them. Now they may have cost him his very life!

The rifle leapt up like a live thing and the

Kid flipped a .44 from its holster and drilled a bullet through his heart and out his backbone.

'It's surely a mortal shame to be just too damned good at your job,' he said mockingly, springing nimbly to a lower boulder. He crouched low behind a rock shoulder at the sound of climbing feet. Alerted to the danger by the lurking buzzards, Cobain had waited a patient hour back in the draw with his own field glasses playing over the devil's marbles until he knew exactly how many of the enemy were positioned here, and how he would deal with them.

First take out the top man with the field glasses, then his partner down below would either run or climb.

He was counting on the latter outcome, and couldn't help but grin in self-satisfaction as he listened to the laboured breathing, the scrape of boot leather on rock.

A shadow fell before him. The Kid's twin revolvers were sprouting from his nimble hands as he rose in a half-crouch and opened fire with twin barrels in a continual rolling roar. Struck brutally in torso and head half a dozen times at point-blank range, Cody, the small-time badman, was slammed backwards to drop and roll ten feet before finally coming to rest, looking like something that had fallen off a meat wagon.

'Sure does feel good when it's done right,' Cobain panted. He deftly reloaded as he sprang to ground and headed back for the draw where Maybell placidly waited in the whispering knee-high grass.

## CHAPTER 5

## THE KID CAME TO TOWN

Longley rubbed his left hand along his smoothly shaven jaw then tilted his hat forward to cut down the glare.

From atop a broken-backed ridge not far from the beginnings of the brush country, he had a panoramic view of the sprawling landscape surrounding him. Using the field glasses, he overlooked nothing – no crevice, draw, rock pile, shadow or change of colour or texture.

It was late the following day as he scouted some ten miles north-east of the camp ground. He'd just found something but wasn't sure if it was important – a scatter of boot and hoof prints in the lee of a rocky overhang that had protected the sign a little from the Kree winds.

He'd been in the saddle twenty hours straight ever since the Kid returned from the Slot. He and Morell had ridden immediately back to the shoot-out site to find the night critters already feasting. Morell didn't recognize the dead, but both agreed the pair had the look of town toughs who'd do most anything if the price was right.

The only town anywhere near the Sawteeth Range was Crow Creek lying some fifteen miles to the northeast of his present position out on the plateau sweeps.

Morell interpreted the Slot shoot-out as proof that their original assumption or guess – Joe still wasn't sure which – that the horse gang had struck north from Stud Ranch, was dead on target.

Who else but a bunch on the run would stake out the passes with hellers with guns? he'd asked rhetorically, and Vallance had reached his conclusions when they got back to camp.

Prior to the bloody gundown, Joe had figured in his hard-nosed practical way that, whatever Vallance's posse might be doing, it just didn't add up that it was only hunting horse-thieves. But he'd been willing to do the big man's job and accept his money until he found out the real reason they had come trailing up here, then if he didn't like it, quit.

That didn't hold any longer. Two gunmen had lain in wait to kill the Kid and may well have succeeded had it been anybody but that gunslick. The bloody clash had convinced him they could be up against someone like Chiller. Who else but an outlaw in fear of pursuit would go to the extreme of posting gunmen to watch his back trail with orders to shoot to kill?

Neither of the other two passes had revealed any sign of recent activity. It seemed plain that Chiller – still assuming he was behind it – had figured a posse would select the best entrance to the canyon lands and had deployed his guns accordingly.

Backed by Morell, Longley had ridden through the Slot to reach Twisted Valley, first dramatic sector of the wilderness. There'd been recent rain on the Sawteeth's northern slopes with the result that most prints had been washed away. But there was sufficient left to reveal that well-mounted men had been in the area recently, their tracks arrowing away north-west in the general direction of Prophet's Well.

Returning to the south side, he'd spent patient hours working his way westward hunting tracks or clues, frustrating hours due to the flimsiness of the soil and the destructive nature of the wind.

But he had picked up some sign at the ridge, which he returned to now.

The muddled blur of prints suggested strongly that the riders who had made them were heading north-east, possibly making in the direction of Crow Creek.

There was something unusual about one fading bootprint that he wanted to check out.

Climbing a little higher back up on to the ridge, he gazed out over the miles of grey-green brush and sketched a map in his mind of the route he would follow through the vegetation, were he intending to get to the town from this point.

Once this track was clear in his mind he filled leather and came down off the ridge, soon to be swallowed by the brush.

He rode every yard with his eyes on the ground. The Kree Plains were notorious for their high summer winds. It was blowing now, and glancing back, he saw his own hoofprints already beginning to fill with sand. But he kept on until, through the tangled brush ahead, he glimpsed the terrain change he'd noted from the ridge.

Here on rising ground there grew heavier trees, old oaks and wind-tortured pines forming a natural barricade against the winds. Riding between the sturdy old trunks he noted progressively more earth and less sand, much of it held together by matted pine needles.

When he finally emerged he found the earth beneath him was mainly just that. Earth. And even from the back of his horse he could make out the hoof tracks left by two horsemen making in the direction of an out-of-sight wagon trail to the town.

He followed the sign at a lope for several miles before finding what he was looking for.

The riders had halted here to smoke, water their horses – and leave prints. Two medium to large men wearing solid bootwear and smoking good tobacco, were the assessments he made in moments. It took a little longer to find a good print of the larger man's boot which sported a rowel spur. He knelt and blew sediment from the print and examined it for a minute before giving a soft grunt of satisfaction.

The spur had one broken tooth.

This was the characteristic he'd suspected in the sign back at the ridge, while the size and shape of the boot-heel was, he was equally certain, the same print he'd come across not far from the Slot.

Suddenly he had himself a lead.

A man who'd been at the Slot and then ridden this way was making for Crow Creek and Longley was next door to certain he could identify him if they caught up with him.

He jumped to his feet and trotted back to his horse.

He was ready for some fun – for a change.

He stood on the step of the True West Hotel sporting a new store-bought white shirt buttoned carefully to the top, which was held with a little gold stud on which was engraved a tiny red rose. The conservative shirt was offset by striped twill pants – a form of insurance against going unnoticed – and there was a feather in his hatband that had come from a buzzard at the spot where he'd grabbed himself some gun glory and earned himself a handsome Vallance bonus into the bargain.

He was bathed, smiling and already

drawing attention on this quiet Crow Creek back street, the complete picture of some flashy young stranger looking to avail himself of whatever diversions their town might have to offer, but for one thing.

The eyes.

Kid Cobain's eyes could sparkle, sulk or smile, but the glitter lurking in their depths was never quite subdued. They held the dark intensity of a boy barely a man who lived with death and laughed about it.

He came down off the gallery with a light step and an easy smile, thinking, 'What a dump!' Working joes, stumbling bums, fat men in silk waistcoats and big-breasted matrons passing by like pouter pigeons eyeing him suspiciously from beneath their parasols. 'Howdy there, Ma'am. Anybody interesting creeping into your bed reeking of whiskey and randy as a polecat these long summer nights, hmm? Reckon not, somehow, but never give up hope for the Kid is here. Alleluia!'

He chuckled out loud, attracting the attention of a passer-by. The man frowned and the Kid tipped his hat. 'How do, Father. Would you be so good as to direct me to the nearest purveyor of fermented liquors?'

'Huh...?'

'Much obliged. Give my regards to Mr Vallance when he comes looking for me.'

The towner moved on, bewildered, and Cobain executed a little dance step upon the weathered walk. He sure was in good form this evening, which he reckoned was more than could be said for old moneybags Vallance.

They'd tried to stop him when he suddenly decided he'd spent enough time waiting for Longley to show, jumped atop Maybell and headed for the town. They had no chance. He was ready for a little relaxation and nobody out there could argue that he hadn't earned it.

Of course he knew where the saloon was. He'd stopped off for a heart-starter before going off to find a wash-house, barber and gentleman's outfitter in that order.

The Chaparral House consisted of a barroom that was eighty feet long by forty wide. Big heavy couches covered with buffalo robes stood along the walls. The same booze-hounds who'd been slumped on them when he'd arrived before were still there when the Kid swaggered in and called for whiskey in a voice just a little too loud.

The massive roof beams over his head were stained almost black by smoke; Indian blankets were scattered across the hard-packed earthen floor. From each rude beam hung a bronze lamp. There was a big sign behind the bar that read:

In God we trust – others pay cash.

The Kid paid his cash and crossed the room to where two girls, one tall and skinny, her companion small and elfin, sat in their tawdry finery upon a couch sipping whiskey and water from coloured glasses.

'Baby,' he smiled at the pretty one, showing all his teeth, 'I'm here to tell you your lonesome days are over.' He extended his hand. 'Let's dance.'

'But ... but there's no music,' she stammered, yet rising all the same.

'Wrong.' Her hand in his, he swung to face the curious crowd. He snapped his fingers. 'Music. C'mon, c'mon, a man doesn't have all day. Can't you see a lady's waiting to dance with her feller?'

Some seemed ready to cheek him back, but others, wiser and more perceptive, just stood in silence looking uneasy as the stranger stood there with that big empty smile that looked as if it could switch off like a light. Then one drew a harmonica from his pocket, managed to blow a tune through it, and another began slapping time on the bartop with his hands.

Good enough, decided the Kid.

The young couple glided round and round and hard men made room for them, for reasons they weren't quite sure – yet they made plenty of room.

That was how it started.

An hour's dancing led to supper at the diner next door followed by a stroll in the twilight – a killer in a white shirt and a hard-time girl in buttons and bows – and yet they could have been innocent young lovers, and the Kid was certainly talking like one.

He figured he didn't have much time to play the gallant, get her into bed and then get rid of her. After that, maybe, just maybe, he'd be ready to listen to whoever they sent in to get him, and they would send somebody.

He hoped it might be Morell. He'd stick it up to that sonuva before agreeing to go back with him. He'd enjoy that.

'This might be the sweetest night of my whole life, Emmaline,' he declared as they passed by the lamplit general store. 'You're beautiful, I'm dyin' to live ... it's a perfect night. Hell, even the poor folks are beautiful tonight, just lookit.'

The peasant family in the dog cart looked lumpy and ugly at a distance, but as they drew closer and the street lamp found them they were revealed as a young couple with two wide-eyed children in clean working clothes who stared wide-eyed and admiring at the flashy town couple on the walk before passing on.

'Just plain folks,' commented the Kid. 'But salt of the earth and all four of them Heaven bound, I swear to God.'

She loved the way he talked and he loved everything about her. Sure, he knew it wouldn't last, and couldn't. But while it did, whether it be for hours or a mere fleeting minute, tonight he was just an everyday kind of feller and she was his blushing, sweet-scented sweetheart and nothing could touch them.

It was a rare moment that saw the Kid come even close to relaxing. Tonight was one such time. This might have been the reason he didn't notice the gaunt man with the moustache staring out of the hash-house window, but the man certainly saw him.

Morell glanced back over his shoulder.

'You can pick up some, Longley. We're not going to a funeral, y'know.'

Riding two horse-lengths behind, Longley gave no sign he'd heard. Ahead with Morell rode Santone and Flagg on their big grain-fed quarter horses. Dalton trailed Longley with the big double buggy churning along behind, throwing dust against the stars.

'You hear what I said, mister?'

Morell was testy. He'd been gripped by a powerful sense of misgiving ever since returning to camp from reconnoitre, only to find that Longley was still away scouting while the Kid had taken himself off to town.

It was an hour before Longley showed, by which time Morell had the party ready to pull out.

Cobain's work out at the Slot had convinced Morell he'd been right in pressing for the killer's selection in the posse. But admiration in no way blinded his judgment. He regarded the Kid as an artist of the .44s, most likely the deadliest guntipper of them all, yet unpredictable and flawed.

Their task here wasn't half completed and Morell didn't want to get to Crow Creek and discover that Cobain had either quit, got lost or maybe shot the mayor – if they had town mayors up here on the rim of the great wilderness. They had to hurry before any of that happened, so why was Longley dragging the chain?

Times like this, wasn't it reasonable to

expect teamwork?

He leaned back in the saddle to slow his horse, enabling Longley to draw abreast. The Tadpole man was still travelling at the same steady lope.

'You looking to go to sleep in the saddle, Farmer?'

'Not unless you are – Lonely.'

Morell cursed. 'We must be sicker than we look. Now we're cussing one another with that lousy little scut's nicknames!'

'You hate his guts, don't you?'

'Sure. Everybody does.'

'Then why wear out horseflesh rushing to town? He can look after himself.'

Morell's jaw muscles worked. He ducked his head beneath a leaning lamp, tugged down his hat.

'Thought I made myself clear on that, damnit. I just told you this job isn't finished. We'll need him worse once we move into the wilderness than before ... so we can't risk losing him.'

The cavalcade drummed onwards for a minute before Longley replied.

'We calculate Chiller's around six-men strong, right?'

'So?'

'There's eight of us not counting the Kid.

We've been travelling less time than Chiller and four of us are guns for hire. Don't you figure that gives us an edge even without Cobain?'

'Mebbe,' the other replied, looking away.

Longley studied the gunman's clean-cut profile. They worked well together. That was as far as it went, but it was enough. They'd come to half-trust one another and it irked him when he felt Morell wasn't levelling.

He glanced back at the rig as it jounced over a tree root in the road. Back there, seated up behind Clancy on his heat seat, were two others who treated him with respect yet kept holding something back.

He turned to the way ahead, chiselled features flinty now.

This was a dangerous job of work; the Slot shoot-up had proven that. They might haul Cobain out of Crow Creek without more trouble, but there was no guarantee on that. Now it seemed certain that Morell, Vallance and Webb were expecting dangerous days ahead of them if the manhunt continued into the wilderness, yet he was expected to accept that prospect despite the fact that they still didn't trust him enough to tell him the whole truth.

Well, he had news for them. If they didn't

square with him in Crow Creek he would kiss the rest of his contract money goodbye, and they could go find themselves a new scout who both knew the stone country and wasn't afraid of it.

And good luck to them!

The hush of an August night lay upon Crow Creek. Lights still burned but even the Chaparral House seemed quieter than usual, hardly anybody on the streets, everything peaceful under the vast black sky.

But along at the rooming-house on the side street an outlaw named Hatch sat on the back step to catch whatever breath of air there was, grinding his teeth and every now and then spitting bad-tempered curses or taking a swig from his brandy flask.

Suddenly the door behind him swung open with a bang and Roth appeared, grinning, shucking out of his coat, anything but repentant.

'Landlady says you've been waiting–'

'Where in Hades have you been?' demanded Hatch, on his feet and truculent. He waved his arms. 'We're here on a quick stopover... I've been waiting for you for two hours.'

'OK, OK, don't blow a valve.' Sugar Lee

Roth was a rawboned redhead with an easy-going manner that was deceptive. He peered at his partner closely. 'You look twitchy,' he said soberly. 'What is it?'

'Kid Cobain is what.'

Roth stared.

'What are you talking about?'

'He's here in town. I've never seen the son of a whore before but I've seen his likeness often enough.' A wild and craggy-headed man who looked as if he'd never slept under a roof, Hatch threw his long arms wide. 'It's him sure enough. Strutting around like a peacock and smooching one of the jades from the Chaparral. I damn near walked over that weaner on the sidewalk. So, what's the betting the mystery of what happened to our hardcases out at the Slot ain't so much of a puzzle any more, huh?'

Roth's eyes were mean as sin. Like his trail partner, he was a denizen of the outlaw trails: weathered, dangerous, a quick and merciless killer. He caressed the handle of his belt gun with spatulate fingers. He was digesting the other's information, and spotted a way of taking it forward another step.

'Well, we could tell right off them killin's had to be the work of a pro ... which fits that bastard like a glove...' he said musingly. He snapped his fingers. 'Hey! You reckon the Kid could've tracked you and me back from the Slot after we found them carcasses?'

'Reckon not. We were mighty careful with the sign, remember? Besides, I ain't sure he'd have had time. The bastard's been here hours. If you'd have been around–'

'Yeah, yeah, get over it.' Roth began pacing to and fro, frequently darting glances at the surrounding gloom, edgy but not scared. Red Hatch and Sugar Lee Roth had ridden with Chiller's outlaw gang for better than two years, the hardest school in the hardest of all trades.

Roth finally quit stepping it out and hauled a long-barrelled Frontier Model Colt .45 to double-check the loads.

'We know that bunch has been dogging us for days,' he stated calmly. 'We figured we could stop them at the Sawteeth, might've done it but for Cobain ... I'm damn certain it was that mucker now.' He clicked his piece closed and slid it into his belt holster, stroking the octagonal barrel lovingly. He stared off towards the central block, tight white creases etching the stubble at the corners of his mouth. 'And now he's ours, Red....'

'What do you mean – ours? You're not thinkin'–'

'Not thinking, man, *doing*.' He clapped a hand to Hatch's shoulder, squeezed hard. 'Look, don't you see? That butchering son of a whore has made a slip-up. He don't know we're here, we'd likely be dead if he did. He's come in to flash it up and maybe grab some tail, and right now he's likely kicking back someplace soaking it up, could even be sleeping – killing can be tiring work, you know? So what are we waiting for? Just picture Ned's face when we tell him we got their butcher boy.'

'Yeah... right!' suddenly Hatch was picturing. The other's confidence was infectious. With deliberate slowness he reached down and drew his own belt gun from the soft leather holster snugged to his right hip. The weapon came clear with a soft hiss. It was a splendid Colt 1861 converted from cap-and-ball to cartridges. It was an outdated weapon but beautifully balanced. It had been decorated with brass and butt plates of amber.

He lifted his eyes to the other's and they nodded grimly before going off to look for the Kid.

# CHAPTER 6

## ANGELS AND ASSASSINS

Bathed in the glow of a low-burning lantern and naked as God made them, lying there upon the rumpled bed in her cubby-shack in the saloon yard, they looked not at all like a killer and a two-dollar whore, more like angels, slender and beautiful angels loving one another exactly as their creator had intended all mankind to do, even the good, the bad and the very bad indeed.

He fitted the latter rating to a tee, yet tonight the Kid was still firmly in the grip of one of his most prolonged periods of sweetness and light, where no murderous demons or nightmare rages could even be remembered, much less be allowed to intrude and overtake him as had happened so often in the past.

He was the boy, she the girl, and all he really needed to make it perfect was another smooth jolt of that fine blended bourbon from the bottle resting on the flimsy bedside chair.

Stirring gently in order not to disturb her half-sleep, he reached for the bottle and froze. He might be relaxed but his senses were never less than razor-sharp, no matter what the circumstances. In that moment he realized, maybe belatedly, that there was something amiss – sight, sound, scent. He didn't even know what it was as yet, only that the hair on the back of his neck never lifted that way unless something was in the wind.

He snatched up his gunbelt, killed the light and hit the floor in a lightning exhibition of explosive animal reflexes that saw the .45 slug intended for his heart thud harmlessly instead into the mattress where he'd lain a split-second before.

In the same instant the girl sprang up and dived instinctively for the door, striking it hard and vanishing through it like a white wraith in animal panic – so obviously not the victim the shadowy killers were hunting that she didn't even attract a single slug as she rushed blindly away, too frightened even to scream, waist-length hair flying. The men with the guns knew who they wanted here.

There was now a jagged-edged hole in the tiny window where moments before a two-inch gap in the faded curtains had enabled the gunman outside to draw a bead on the man he wanted dead.

Sprawled upon the floor with every nerve end jangling, the wild-eyed Kid's first instinct was to follow the girl through the slowly-closing door, maybe somersault roll once or twice to confuse them, then open up and chop the bastards down as only he might. But the gun that suddenly came thrusting through the broken window to spew great gouts of shimmering yellow flame into the smoky room saw him instead hold his precarious place as understanding struck home.

He was up against real pros!

Triggering back, he dived beneath the bed, wincing as a lead hornet raked his calf before shattering a chair leg into splinters that peppered his naked flesh like angry scorpions.

Two of them! he realized now. One using the window, the other pumping lead through the flimsy walls at random, their shouts drowning out the screams as the fleeing girl finally found her voice.

The entire life-or-death sequence had occupied but moments, so swift had been both the actions and reactions of all four involved.

Jaws locked and snarling like a dog, Cobain raised his gun hand above the bed and emptied a whole chamber through the window in one uninterrupted rolling roar before realizing he didn't have his shell belt, that he couldn't afford to waste bullets.

In short – as retaliatory lead came searching for him again – he was trapped like a rat and left with but one hope of survival.

'Help!' he howled, scarcely able to believe it was his voice he heard struggling to rise above the thunder of guns and the flat whacking sounds of bullets slamming flimsy walls. 'These bastards are trying to murder me. Somebody out there. Do something! Help!'

The two wide-shouldered men hurrying along the wide street in the direction of the gunshots halted momentarily at the sound of the high-pitched voice punctuating the gunfire.

Their eyes locked and held for the shaved tip of a second, each mirroring the same thought. Was that a familiar voice? Could it be...?

Morell was first to shake his head. 'That one would rather die than holler uncle!' he panted. 'But you can bet your last buck this gunplay's got some connection with him. I said we should've hurried.'

'Keep your shirt on,' Longley snapped back, shooting a glance over his shoulder as they started off again.

Behind them were citizens holding on to their hats as if ready to break and run if the trouble should spill over into the street. Further back out front of the True West Hotel, the rest of their party were milling round the buggy as Vallance and Webb climbed down. At the sudden eruption of gunfire, Morell had ordered Santone, Dalton and Flagg to stay close to the big man while they checked the scene.

The shouting had subsided, but a rifle-toting Longley still reckoned it had been the Kid they'd heard.

A naked blonde came rushing from the long, narrow alley as they approached, arms flailing wildly, 'Save him, for God's sake – he didn't do anything!'

'Looks like he might've done something,' Morell panted as, shoulder to shoulder, they raced to the alley's end and found them-selves in the dimly lit rear yard of the saloon, some hundred feet from the two shadowy figures pumping shots into a fragile-looking cubby-shack that seemed to be rocking on its supports.

Then two shots erupted from within the cubby accompanied by a maniacal snarl: 'You'll never count coup on me you motherless sons of bitches ... I'll finish myself before I'd ever let any tenth-rater do that!'

That was the moment both Longley and Morell knew it was indeed the Kid; couldn't be anyone else.

'Hold up!' Morell shouted. 'Drop those guns and get 'em up over your h–'

The response was lightning, the reaction of real men of the gun. In an instant the two had sprung behind the cubby, cursing, shooting and already backing away into the darkness enshrouding a vast liveoak.

A slug droned past Longley's ear and he jerked the trigger of the rifle. There was a sharp cry of pain, a curse, three more wilder shots then the rush of running feet.

'I got a hunch I know who those bastards are!' Morell yelled, starting after them. 'We can't let them get away.'

They were rushing by the cubby when the bullet-riddled door jerked open and the tousled head of Kid Cobain appeared around it. He recognized them and jumped out, bird-naked and clutching two empty .44s.

'Hold up, Lonely!' he shouted. 'Wait till I

get some bullets, a hoss an … and some god-damn pants. Hold up, I said, you bastards!'

But fast-moving Longley and Morell were already gone, engulfed momentarily by the darkness enshrouding the huge old tree then bursting into the narrow laneway, just as two dark figures, one running freely and the other limping badly, left it fifty yards further on.

The pair followed fast. Longley wasn't questioning anything. When you rode for a brand you did what was expected of you. It was plain as paint that Morell intended to deal with the Kid's antagonists, and wondered if he mightn't be able to guess just who Morell reckoned they could be.

Hoofbeats stuttered before they could make it from the alley into the back yard of the livery where quick clouds of dust were rising behind two horses leaping away from a tierail.

Morell dropped to one knee and fanned gun hammer with a smooth unhurried motion. A man cried out in pain, two bullets came screaming back, the riders boiled round a corner and were gone.

Nobody attempted to interfere as Longley and Morell rushed into the livery, led two startled mounts from their stalls, snatched bridles off a saddle tree, sprang astride bareback and went charging out into the night at a surging gallop.

'Bastards!'

They figured it was the Kid but whether it was or wasn't didn't signify. They couldn't see any riders in the street they swung into but the dust was their ally, and when they reached the first corner, took it at full pace and straightened up, there were the fast-running horsemen some two hundred yards ahead storming towards the bridge.

As they stormed after them, Morell housed his cutter and yelled over his shoulder, 'I'm as good as certain these muckers ride with Chiller! So keep that claybank moving – Farmer!'

'Whatever you say – Lonely!'

Vallance set a cigar between his teeth and waited for someone to light it. Webb obliged, flicking the dead vesta into the cuspidor by the bar. The rancher inhaled deeply and glanced at the batwings, then up at the clock above the bar.

'An hour gone,' he growled. 'Why didn't Morell check with me to say if they should go after those gunners. Most likely I'd have said no.'

'He'd have his reasons, Mr Vallance.'

Seated before a tall glass of sarsaparilla, Webb seemed about the only denizen of the Chaparral House unaffected by the shoot-out. It was the chief topic of conversation throughout the smoke-filled bar-room, and even Vallance's hard men, Santone, Dalton and Flagg were acting edgy, watching the doors, windows and their fellow drinkers with suspicion.

'Perhaps.' Vallance was a large and robust man with polished manners and a deal of iron in his make-up. 'I guess we're lucky that he's got Longley with him. There's more to that fellow than you first think. And he did excellent work today, picking up on that sign the way he did....' He watched the cigar smoke climbing towards the rafters. 'Maybe that was them after all...'

'Them?' hard-eyed Santone queried. 'What *them?*'

'Well, Longley's convinced the two men he tracked out of the Sawteeths to this dump were also at the Slot,' the rancher supplied. 'And two men jumped Cobain. If it was the same two it would make sense Morell chasing off after them if he calculated that perhaps they are with Chiller. What do you say, Webb?'

Before Webb could reply there was a bad-tempered rap of bootheels on the long porch before the batwings flew apart and the Kid came in.

He propped and glared round the room, his eyes flaring cold.

'Well, what does everyone think they're looking at – you monkey-faced jackass sons of bitches?'

This was aggressive even by the Kid's standards. Glances dropped away and the bartender began wiping down with a jerky, nervous motion. Only the men at Vallance's table held the new arrival's off-focused stare. They were with Mr Big; they were also the most dangerous men in town – Vallance's hand-picking of his possemen had seen to that.

Cobain seemed to ease off a notch when his words drew no response. He looked a far cry from the young man who'd been seen escorting a girl around town earlier. His fine white shirt was grubby, his hair was wild and he had strapping round his right leg where he'd been injured in the shoot-out.

'So,' Webb said after a silence, his voice toneless. 'You're back. Any luck?'

The Kid turned his head and spat. By the time he'd gotten dressed and found his horse, both the men who'd attempted to sack his saddle and Longley and Morell had vanished out along the trail to the wilderness. He'd spent half an hour searching for sign, twenty minutes cursing, then galloping back to town in a fury.

He'd been jumped by genuine gunmen and had survived. That would have been enough to make most men feel pretty good. But the Kid wasn't most men. It was his towering vanity that had taken the real beating tonight. Staring death in the eye, he'd been forced to resort to yelling for help. Not many had heard, yet he believed every citizen and his dog had done so. Had he caught so much as a whisper, a snigger or a knowing look it might have proven difficult even for Vallance to hold him back.

Luckily there was nobody suicidally inclined in that taut minute, and then he jerked off his hat, slapped a great cloud of dust off his pants and came across to the table to snatch up Flagg's glass and drain it.

Flagg made to rise but Santone's sharp word saw the man resume his seat.

'Just what do they think they are?' the Kid hissed, hooking a chair with his toe then dropping into it. 'I mean, taking off after those John Does thataway. I told them to wait for me. We'll be lucky to see either of those losers again. I mean, those sons that came after me were the real thing. Hotshots. They'd eat old Lonely and the Farmer whole, if they fluked running them down.'

'Who were they, Kid?' asked Vallance. 'We're wondering if they could be with our horse-thieves.'

'Could be, I guess.' Cobain was quietening. He'd burned up a lot of coal tonight. But he was still sore. 'I can go see if I can track them at first light?'

'We'll wait and see how Joe and Morell make out,' Vallance replied. 'Who knows? They could get lucky. If your friends are with Chiller, Kid, and if the boys could take those hardcases alive, we might just be able to persuade them to take us to where the gang's holing up ... to my horse.'

'Who cares about your h–?' Cobain began, but caught himself in time. Vallance was his conduit to a big pay day and quite possibly the thing he craved most: glory. The theft of Vallance's famed horse was still major news throughout the south-west. The newspapers were following the manhunt closely, poised to trumpet the outcome all over the territory, whether it be good or bad.

A perfect result in the Kid's eyes would see

him in at the kill and vindicating Vallance's confidence in him by blasting Lucky Ned and most of his bunch into oblivion. After that nobody would talk about Territory gun wizards in general. There'd just be him up there. The Kid.

The girl came in with her friend. She started towards Cobain who greeted her with such a remote and icy hostility that she flushed hotly and sensibly turned away.

He barely saw her. He was writing headlines in his mind.

They approached the ghostly silhouette of the butte in midnight gloom with barely enough starlight to see where they were putting their feet. When they reached the suddenly looming bulk of the lightning-split oak they deployed wordlessly, then closed again when beyond the tree to within a hundred feet apart, Morell easing off towards the huge piles of talus at the base of the butte as Longley circled wider in the open.

Joe held his rifle loosely with his finger on the trigger. He was adept with a six-shooter but had greater confidence in the Winchester. He paused to sniff, his wilderness-trained senses sifting, analysing, testing. There were all sorts of wild and animals scents in the air out here, close by the vast grey lava beds that marked out the beginning of the Burning Stone wilderness. He wasn't interested in any landmarks; not when he could also detect the smell of horse, gun oil, tobacco and maybe blood.

The gunmen's luck had begun to sour several miles back when one of their horses tore a tendon, causing them to double up on the other. This enabled Longley and Morell to close in then push them hard, until with moonset their quarry had suddenly quit the faint trail and attempted to lose them by travelling cross country.

The ploy had not worked. The double-laden horse had finally given out, leaving them to seek refuge someplace here around the butte.

Joe was sweating. It wasn't the first time he'd hunted the deadliest of all quarry, but a year's ranching could take the edges off a man. Maybe. He counted himself lucky to have Morell with him. He doubted if anyone would ever get remotely close to that hardcase, but he'd proven himself a cool head when the chips were down and this was the quality that counted most.

He paused to catch his breath with ears, nose and eyes all working overtime, before moving on.

He'd taken just two steps that carried him by a waist-high, ghost-grey boulder, when he heard from a patch of deeper shadow off to his right, the tiny, lethal click of a gun hammer being thumbed back.

He dived headlong as the gunshot erupted with a startling crash that was accentuated by the night's deep silences.

He sensed the whipping passage of bullet going by at deadly velocity as he rolled away seeking the safety of the darkness, first kicked this way, then that, his rifle ready to fire the moment he figured the dry-gulcher's position.

Then came the bellow of two shots from a distance followed by a cry of pain close by. Morell had positioned his attacker by his gunflash and responded instantly. He heard the man fall but was immediately forced to duck his head down tight as a fearsome volley of shots erupted from another angle, the machine-gun rapidity of the fire possible only by holding your trigger down tight and fanning the gun hammer.

Then, 'The white rock, Hatch!'

The hoarse shout came from the position where he'd heard a man go down. Longley triggered twice, low. There was an answering shot followed by the scrabble of boots on stone, the echoes of the gunblast making it impossible to figure which direction the quarry was taking.

Then it was Morell's voice coming from the great shroud of darkness back towards the tree. 'Leave them to me, Farmer. No point you getting killed for nothing!'

'Watch your own ass and I'll watch mine!' Anticipating enemy fire, Joe wedged himself between two canting boulders and smiled grimly as the foe retaliated, shots slamming harmlessly into stone above and showering him with fragments.

He was up.

Like a boxer executing a feint in order to draw his adversary where he didn't want to go, Longley scooped up a rock and flung it hard to his left. It struck with a clatter but drew no shots. His jaw muscles worked. Pros. He'd sensed it from the outset when this pair came within an ace of sacking Cobain's saddle.

All his senses were in full battle-mode now. Easing across the face of the butte with no more noise than a passing thought, he was quickly able to position Morell moving in his same general direction maybe fifty yards off to his right. More stealthy sounds and the occasional whiff of scent that only a real man of the wilds could possibly detect, told him that their quarry were moving towards what appeared to be a pear-shaped, light-coloured boulder due west, one sure on his feet, the other dragging.

This took him back to the Mescalero Wars of '72, when it was you or them, none but buzzards to commemorate the occasion if you failed.

There was a shot from Morell's position; he must have seen or heard something.

A curse and a vivid blast of gunpowder close by the boulder was the response.

Instantly Longley fired the Winchester across his body. Despite the flare of his own gunblast, he sensed rather than saw the dark silhouette of a man falling against that backdrop of yellow stone.

He knew the man was dead.

So, it seemed, did the second gunman. Longley could see nothing, but the sounds of receding running steps told him all he needed to know.

'North of the yellow rock!' he bawled at the top of his lungs, and glimpsed the wraith-like silhouette of Morell moving swiftly ahead and to his right. Longley gave the chase everything he had, but both

Morell and the retreating outlaw remained well beyond his range until suddenly he leaned back and allowed bootheels ploughing in the dirt to drag him to a halt.

Two shots, followed by another – then the drumbeat of hoofs quickly fading.

Breathing hard, he prudently dropped to one knee before calling, 'Morell?'

'Lost the bastard,' came the panting response from surprisingly close by. Morell's unmistakable wedge-shaped torso showed dimly. 'Where are you?'

'Here!'

Longley, uncoiling to his full height, allowed his rifle to point to the ground as Morell emerged from the wraith of darkness. He jabbed the barrel towards the pear-shaped boulder, and nodded.

'Other one's yonder.'

'We'd better take it cautious.'

'It's OK, he's dead.'

'How can you be sure?'

'Just am.'

A minute later found them bending over the life-less body of Sugar Lee Roth. The outlaw had his name etched on his gunbelt, but Morell had identified him the moment he lighted a vesta.

'Badman and gunman with his face pasted

on trees halfway to Santa Fe, Longley,' he informed, standing with boots wide-planted feeding shells from his belt into his guns. The grey eyes looked white in the darkness. 'And has been with the Chiller gang for two years.'

'So, we've caught up with them at last.'

'And not before time. How far to the wilderness from here?'

'Just a couple hours' ride.'

'C'mon, let's get our nags. Vallance needs to hear about this.'

'There's lots of things he needs to hear about.'

Morell looked at him sharply. 'Meaning?'

Longley didn't reply. He was striding off in the direction of the horses just as though he could see in the dark.

# CHAPTER 7

## WHY MEN KILL

'Who are you staring at, horse-face?'

The driver of the battered curricle was so startled by the sudden snarl from the young stranger leaning against the bridge pylon, he jerked his donkey to a halt.

'I ... I beg your pardon, young fellow,' he remonstrated, a sunburnt farmer with an honest western face. 'I don't reckon I know you, do I?'

'Everybody knows the Kid, you plough-walking piece of dirt.' Cobain jerked a thumb towards the distant town. 'You just come from the Creek. I say that a mouthy-looking old broken-bones like you would have had to have been swapping lies about me all day long, which means you're just a big-mouthed mucker itching for trouble. Now ain't that the simple truth?'

The farmer had gone grey beneath his summer brown.

'You – you're the one they call the Kid?'

The man sounded guilty, and was. Until today's town visit he'd never heard of Kid Cobain, but they were talking of little else in Crow Creek. On the same morning that two men from the south had returned to report the death of one of the outlaws who'd attempted to murder this man, Cobain had been involved in a series of violent incidents on the streets resulting in two citizens requiring medical treatment, before galloping out of town in a rage some two hours earlier.

Everyone was talking about the Kid. But

this farmer was no fool. He wasn't about to admit it. Cobain looked as crazy as they'd said, and doubly dangerous.

The Kid slouched across to the curricle, thumbs hooked in his belt, a sneer working his hairless lip.

'So, what are they saying about me now, hayseed? That some jade set me up and a brace of tenth-raters tried to do for me? Well, are they?'

The man's heart was in his mouth. Instinct warned him a wrong answer could prove fatal. This man sporting matching revolvers looked like someone who'd snuff a man's life out as indifferently as you would stamp on a cockroach.

'They ... they just said that you ... you got sore on account them other two fellers went chasin' after the outlaws that jumped you, afore ... afore you could scramble into your togs and ride off with 'em, er ... sir. Was that about how it happened, Mr Kid?'

Either the Kid didn't hear or was considering his response. He leaned on the vehicle's rear wheel and stared pensively back towards town for a full minute while the farmer leaked about a pint of cold sweat.

Suddenly he swore, backed up a step and, jerking out a .44 faster than the eye could follow, he crashed two shots into the hot blue sky and howled: 'Yeeehahh! On your way you miserable potato-pickin' son of a b–.'

His words were drowned by the swift clatter of hoofs and thud of wheels on planking as the rig shot away across the bridge, almost capsizing when it hit the rutted road again, the man's shirt-tails flapping as he stood with one boot on the brake and hung on to the reins for dear life.

'Say hello to Hicksville!' the Kid shouted after him but the words faded as though sucked up by the stifling heat.

Lowering the smoking Smith & Wesson he moved to the railing and stared down. The creek was turning like a sluggish brown snake towards the end of a two-hundred-mile journey from the uplands of Utah, the confluence with Yucca River less than a day away south-east.

The Kid's stare was bleak. He spat cotton and broke open the gun. He spun the revolving chamber and slipped in two rounds so there would be five bullets in the gun. He'd seen men shoot their fool legs off loading six bullets. If a man would trust a piece never to go off accidentally then he deserved to get shot.

He put the piece away and walked back to

the mare tethered in the shade of the bridge below. He spoke to her softly and stroked her velvet nose. She nibbled his forgers understandingly. He swore she understood his every mood, even his worst ones, and they didn't come much worse than today.

The killer was so unstable a mere change in wind direction could touch him off on a bad day.

Last night had been a disaster.

For the first time ever he'd allowed himself be jumped by a pair of pros – bird-naked and in a virtually indefensible position.

The situation after the girl had rushed away screaming was so desperate he'd been forced to holler for help, as any man would. But he wasn't just any man. He was the Kid and they were laughing at him, which meant someone had to pay.

The mare grunted and broke into a trot as he vaulted into the saddle and pointed her back towards town.

The peaceful quiet of Crow Creek was deceptive. Longley, outwardly as casual and heat-oppressed as the next man, tramped to the end of the twisted main stem with his Winchester in the crook of his arm then crossed over and tramped right back again.

The walk was working, he realized.

At the end of a long parley with Morell, Webb and Vallance during which the violent events of the night had been reviewed and examined in detail, certain deductions had been made and conclusions reached.

All were in complete agreement now that the Chiller guns were the men Longley had tracked all the way from the Slot; that in all probability they'd been alerted to Cobain's presence here by chance and tried to take him out, failed, then ran for cover.

Result? One dead outlaw in Sugar Lee Roth, and the almost certainty that Lucky Ned and his thieving bunch – plus the prize stallion of the south-west – had to be within reach.

Naturally Vallance was elated and was launching into an outline of their pursuit plan when Longley interrupted to drop his bombshell.

He'd just killed a man in his capacity as scout and Vallance employee, he reminded soberly. That man had subsequently been identified as a notorious killer. But by this Longley no longer now believed that the badmen were confined to just one side in this saga. He made it clear that he considered several of Vallance's own 'possemen' also slotted neatly into that same shadowy category – Kid Cobain for sure.

Nobody denied his words. Nobody said anything. They suspected their scout had more to say. And they were right.

Longley continued. He'd first made these observations as a prelude to bluntly declaring that he could no longer accept that the hunt expedition was anything like a simple search-find-and-retrieve operation, as it had been represented to him at the beginning. He accused Vallance, Webb and probably also Morell of holding out on him, hence his ultimatum.

By the time he paused to take out the makings he had their undivided attention. For a long, thick moment there was only the sound of breathing in the room, the creak of leather as they watched him steadily. The sound of muted footsteps came from outside. Somewhere in the next block, some halfwit was tormenting a dog and making it bark.

Joe took a strong pull on his quirley and summed up where he stood, exactly. They could come clean about such matters as Vallance's reasons for paying out such large sums of money as well as the reason he'd hired gunmen rather than possemen. He challenged the breeder to unveil the mysteries surrounding the whole affair that he'd sensed almost from the outset, otherwise he would be pointing his horse's nose for home by nightfall.

The three had not taken it well; there was any amount of anger and accusation. But calm quickly prevailed when they realized that Longley in a stubborn mood was something that required dealing with, not dismissing.

'I've a feeling you just lost your new ranch house and fittings, Joe,' Morell confided as they left Vallance to consider his ultimatum. 'Too bad. We make a good team, don't you figure?'

'I'm a rancher. I don't team up with gun-sharks.'

'You did the killing last night.'

Longley's jaws worked as he considered the bald truth in that statement.

He couldn't deny it.

They'd gone after a pair of seasoned owlhoots, put one in the ground and driven the other to flight. They had indeed worked well in tandem. But he refused to make any more of that than the simple fact both were experienced scouts, and it would be strange if they didn't coordinate well with bullets

122

whistling round their ears.

The shooting of Roth didn't weigh upon him too heavily. A trailsman who took on jobs like this accepted danger as part of the deal. Chiller's gun dog wasn't the first killer he'd put in the ground and maybe wouldn't be the last, depending on Vallance's decision.

To divert his heavy thoughts he paused in front of a butcher's shop. The sawdust on the floor was new and clean. The butcher in the leather apron was thoughtfully whetting his big knife, a side of beef hanging on a hook behind him. The fellow looked up, saluted him. Joe scowled and moved on. Even if killing could be part of the game, he didn't believe a man should ever get kudos for it.

Longley wondered if eighteen months on Tadpole had swung the scales, that he was now more rancher than wilderness scout.

He halted to look back. The sun was still an hour above the western rim. Out there lay the wilderness and he could hear it calling. It would be lying to say he hoped Vallance might be riled enough by his ultimatum to decide to pay him out. Having come this far, and certain now the horse-thieves were seeking seclusion in the stone country, he had a yearning to see it all again.

The vast and dream-like valleys, the rivers winding their way through chasms they'd carved over millions of years; the breathless spaces and cathedral quiet of places with names such as Stone Forest, the Angel Spires and Dead Man's Grotto.

He shrugged philosophically. If he didn't get there it only meant it wasn't his time to go. He would survive. But he would survive a lot easier with a cup of that raw whiskey they served in cracked crockery cups at the eatery two doors down from the True West. It was a far cry from the old Monongahela rye that he could only ever afford at Christmas. But it was damn fine whiskey with a decent masculine kick that should completely erase images of a dead man lying out under the sky ten miles north-west.

The Kid sighted him as he crossed the street from the hitch-rack out front of the assay office for the livery where a bald man puffing a pipe was examining the hoofs of a forlorn-looking claybank.

The savage mood that had been riding the Kid all day still had him in its grip as he sat sprawled in a sag-bottomed chair on the porch of the general store. Trouble was, he craved trouble to help him slough off the loss of face suffered overnight when he'd

124

lain hollering, naked and scared beneath a flimsy bed in a whore's cubby shack with bullets pounding the furniture into sawdust all about him.

And here was one of the two 'heroes' who'd come to his rescue.

The bastard!

Longley didn't see him until too late. He slowed, then came on as the slight, silky-moving figure propelled himself out of the chair and leaned against a porch support, chewing a match with exaggerated jaw movement.

'Where you heading, hero?'

Joe halted. 'The hash house. Coming?'

'You'd like that, wouldn't you, Farmer Joe? I mean, with an audience, you could tell your big story all over again – and you ain't never going to get weary of that one, are you?'

'What story would that be?'

The Kid's eyes snapped wide. 'You being smart with me, sodbuster?'

'Just asked a question is all.'

'Is that a fact? Well, let me ask you one. You think it makes you some kind of a hot-shot chasing some bums outta town and fluking one with your old squirrel gun, don't you?'

He shrugged. 'Just did what needed doing.'

Cobain spat the pick from his mouth and hitched at his gunbelt. Longley couldn't help but notice just how big and menacing that matched pair of .44s appeared. During the push north he'd heard stories from men who knew about such things, about just what this man – scarcely more than a boy – had done with those weapons, the men he'd killed and maimed. It made him uneasy to wonder if Cobain might be considering adding the name Joe Longley to that list.

'I say it was Morell who bagged that loser, Farmer.'

'Maybe it was.'

'Morell could've done it. He's a top shootist, for a scheming and shifty-eyed operator I wouldn't trust to carry grits to a bear, that is. But you? Buffalo dust! What beats me is why you two would want to cook up a story like that. You and old Lonely up to some double play here, rube? I mean, Vallance is some kind of daddy big-bucks, that's for sure. Is that it? You two cooking up some double play to take the big man down? Something that might work better if Morell takes a back step and pushes you up front? That the caper?'

Longley licked his lips. The Kid was

serious, yet was talking crap. Maybe he was loco? He'd heard the brooding Santone hint at that possibility once or twice.

'Look, Cobain, I'm just a trail scout. I can't outsmart the fox that's been taking my chickens, much less a big-time breeder and rancher like Mr Vallance. It's been fine talking to you, but I'm starving, dry and–'

'I don't like you, Farmer.'

There it was. The Kid's voice had changed and his stare turned ice-cold. It didn't even begin to make sense that the man should brace him over virtually nothing, but was certainly leading up to something.

Imperceptibly the Winchester muzzle began to rise. He would defend himself even if it was hopeless. A tight little fixed smile played at the corners of Cobain's mouth. Slim hands hung loose at gunbutts. His crazy stare said he was planning on giving Longley the ghost of a hope for a moment, then shoot him down like a dog.

'Hey! There you are, Joe. Been looking for you all over.'

The Kid was livid as he pivoted to face the stalwart figure of Morell striding along the puncheons. In an instant the gunman's irrational anger was transferred from one man to the other.

'You just can't help playing hero, can you, Morell?' he mouthed. 'A blind man could see me and your hero buddy have got something cooking here, yet you just had to horn in on account you reckon you're just another big hero after last night too, ain't you?'

Morell was good. He didn't falter. The easy smile never left his face as he halted and spread his hands. 'Hey, ruckusing is just your way of passing time in this dead burg, right, Kid? I don't blame you. I'll be glad to see the back of Crow Creek myself. And I figure you will too when you hear this, Joe. Mr Vallance wants to see you right away.' He winked. 'Could be he's decided to level up with you after all, huh?'

The Kid flushed hotly. His moment was slipping from his grasp. He whirled to face Longley only to see that the diversion had enabled him to raise the Winchester those vital extra inches. He now stared down the .32 barrel that looked like a howitzer at close range. Joe's finger was curled around the trigger but his easy manner matched Morell's own.

'That's sure good news, Morell,' he said mildly. 'Want to come along, Kid? You might be interested in what Mr Vallance has to say.'

'Cut a vein!' Cobain jumped down to the Street, frustration, uncertainty and impotence chasing one another across his face. He was a high-risk player but knew when the cards were stacked against him. 'Both go cut a vein!' was the best he could come up with, and twitching with emotion, went lunging across the street, cursing a drowsy teamster when he drove his wagon a little too close.

'Sorry to horn in on a private powwow,' Morell remarked drily. 'What was that about?'

'Guess you'd have to ask him,' Longley said. 'C'mon, let's go see the man.'

Vallance, after wolfing a passable steak and a steaming bowl of canned tomatoes in silence, sat back, dabbed at his lips with a napkin then took something from a vest pocket and handed it across to Joe.

'Read that first, Longley. It will save me some unnecessary jawing.'

It was coming on dark. Longley held the clipping close to a coal oil lamp and scanned it. It featured a photograph of a stocky, ugly man identified by the caption as 'Boss Petrie, entrepreneur, breeder of fine horses and Southern Utah's finest son.'

The accompanying two-inch report covered last year's Breeders' Association awards in which the judges proclaimed Robert Vallance winner and his stallion Champion the supreme blood sire in the south-west. That was all.

He passed the cutting back across the cluttered table as the girl came to clear away.

'So?' he said. 'I knew most of this.'

'Certainly you did.'

Vallance produced a golden cigar and Webb was quick with a match. Morell relaxed in his chair and winked at the girl as she arrived with a bottle of wine and glasses. Vallance drew deeply, exhaled.

'What you may not know, however, Joe, is the background to that picture and report.' He leaned back, the most impressive man in the room, and aware of it. 'Petrie and I go back a long way. To cut it short, we've always been rivals in the horse business, intense, bitter rivals. Over the years one seemed to gain the upper hand, then the other. That may have gone on indefinitely until the day my finest mare gave birth to Champion and from that moment on Petrie and his ambitions to become the major breeder in the south-west were dead as the dodo.'

Webb poured wine with his customary deadpan efficiency. Longley sampled his glass. It tasted expensive.

'The awards are held every three years,' Vallance continued. 'I won three years ago and Petrie threw everything he had into turning the tables this year. He spent a fortune improving his blood lines, bribed judges, newspaper editors, opinion-makers ... you name it. I romped in again by the length of the straight and Petrie began making plans – plans of a very different kind...'

'He decided to steal Champion, Longley,' Webb supplied. 'I know it sounds crazy. We thought so when we first heard rumours to the effect. We took additional precautions but they weren't enough. You see, we know Petrie hired the Chiller gang to hit the ranch, and of course he was successful.'

'You look a little incredulous, Joe,' Vallance observed from behind a veil of smoke. 'Can't say I blame you. Anyway, a rustler was mortally hit during the raid on the ranch. He was out of his skull with pain, we gave him whiskey and he spilled his guts. He revealed Petrie had contacted Chiller and they hatched the plan for the gang to steal Champion and run it north out of reach of the law through the wilderness. A great deal of money is involved. I contacted an informant who confirmed the whole affair was a Petrie plan ... although of course nobody was ever to know this.' He paused reflectively. 'That outlaw's confession nailed it down, but I believe I would have smelt Petrie's fine hand in the dirty business in time even without their help.'

'But this sounds loco,' Longley protested. 'How could he expect to get away with it? That stallion's known all over the West.'

'Correct,' said Vallance. 'But Utah is a big place, long way from Stud Ranch. And of course Petrie has no intention of showing it publicly. That would be crazy. But the bloodstock business is as corrupt as any other and there are disreputable breeders who would pay a king's ransom just to have Champion cover their mares. Petrie would naturally improve his own breeding stock from the stallion, and because he's a horse in a million, eventually his progeny would dominate the stud horse business and I would be just an also-ran. That, sir, is the ugly truth of this entire episode.'

Longley slugged down some wine and began rolling a cigarette. He was surrounded by sober and serious faces yet still found it all hard to swallow.

'So, you're saying Chiller is delivering Champion to Petrie in Utah?' he asked after a silence.

'We figure sooner than that, Joe,' supplied Morell. 'They've already covered a hundred miles, which is a long hard road for a finely bred horse. Petrie's spread is roughly eighty to ninety miles more from where we sit now. We don't know this for sure but we reckon they'll meet up someplace in the wilderness where they reason there's no chance of their being caught. We figured this from the jump, which is why I rode up and asked you to work with us, Burning Stone being your special country, that is.'

'You're saying we might have to deal with Petrie as well as the gang if we catch them up?' Longley asked.

'Exactly,' said Webb. 'Now perhaps you understand why we brought along gun-fighters and not simple ranch hands. And, of course, why Mr Vallance agreed to pay you such a very large fee. Only a man of your skill and experience up here can help us from here on in, but I'm sure you're already aware of that.'

'So, there you have my secret, Longley,' Vallance said with a tight smile. 'I feel better now I've cleared the air.'

'Why didn't you tell me at the start?' he asked.

'You might have turned us down,' Morell replied.

'I still might.'

'We hope you don't,' Vallance stated flatly. 'If you were to quit at this late stage it could well mean the difference between success and failure. Will you at least think it over?'

Longley nodded as he rose. He needed time, wasn't sure himself what he might decide. He did know he'd always hated quitting a job unfinished.

'I'll let you know in the morning,' he said and walked out.

It was quiet at the table for a long minute. Then Vallance asked, 'You think he'll stick?'

'I've a hunch he might,' Morell said confidently. Then he frowned. 'But we're going to have to do something about the Kid. I busted up what looked like big trouble brewing between him and Longley earlier ... all over last night. That Kid's half-cracked and—'

'And also indispensable to our mission,' Webb cut in firmly. 'Don't fret about Cobain. Mr Vallance can handle him. It's Longley we're not sure of.'

'Well, we spun him a plausible story,' Vallance drawled, signalling Webb to pour him another. He nodded. 'And he's a decent man, straight. I'm sure he'll decide a decent man should do his duty.'

'By the time he realizes what we really intend to do, Longley will have gotten us to where we want to go,' Webb intoned in a slow voice. He stared fixedly at Vallance. 'But I guess he'll be sore when the coin drops that we're not just after Champion but to put paid to Petrie.'

'Petrie...' Vallance's eyes were fixed on some distant nothingness as he rolled the name round his tongue again.

It had been no ordinary rivalry that existed between him and Petrie; they were anything but ordinary men. Although each wealthy and successful today, their early lives of struggle and rivalry had been totally different. For both were overambitious and violent young men who could have well had their lives cut short by mutual hatred and the reckless risks both had taken in order to reach the top.

Somehow both survived to achieve fame and fortune in maturity in the same line of work in separate territories. But the latent hatred and rivalry had never faded, and the very day Vallance was publicly pronounced top of his field for the second time, Petrie had set out to take by force what he'd been unable to achieve by legitimate means.

Vallance had understood all this when the dying horse-thief revealed Petrie's involvement in the theft of his stallion, and knew that this had to be settled finally this time, once and for all regardless of cost, time or personal danger.

His last great obsession. Get Petrie.

'Petrie...' he said aloud, his emotion naked for all to see. He shook himself and seemed to grow larger and more commanding than they'd ever seen him. His voice took on a forced heartiness: 'No need to worry a decent fellow like Longley by revealing that recovering my beauty, vital though he certainly is, is really only secondary.' He looked up at the erect Webb. 'And what is our primary concern out there in the wilderness, Mr Webb?'

Webb almost smiled.

'Why, to kill Petrie, sir.'

'With what, man, with what?' Vallance barked, his expression suddenly fierce.

'With extreme prejudice, Mr Vallance.'

'You hear that, Morell?' Vallance demanded. 'Extreme goddamned prejudice.'

He laughed suddenly, an almost braying sound. 'And prejudice doesn't come any more extreme than that crazy Kid Cobain.'

## CHAPTER 8

## TO THE BURNING STONE

They descended into the first valley. The scrubby cedar growth began to fail, the bunches of sage growing fewer and farther between. At this point in the journey the wilderness still lay out of sight beyond the rearing ramparts of the range ahead. But Longley could smell it, feel it, was already breathing it. It seemed in his last two years of sod-busting, horse-breaking and coaxing scrawny cattle to add a little extra beef, he'd half-forgotten what the Burning Stone country was really like, the reasons it had always exerted such a fascination for him.

His reverie was interrupted when Morell drew up to ride abreast.

'Another five miles, you figure, Joe?'

'Maybe four.'

Morell pointed ahead. 'I recall that butte,

don't I?'

'Yeah. The outlaws were beginning to play out by the time they got this far.'

Morell hipped around in his saddle to look back. The armed cavalcade travelling in single file along a track that barely passed for a trail, made a reassuring sight against a backdrop of a hillside coated in yellow broomsedge. The screech of a hunting eagle a reminder of the wild country they were entering.

The gunman nodded in satisfaction. He'd chosen his manhunters with care and they were measuring up. They might make lousy company on the trail with such as Santone, Dalton and Flagg preferring to ride and camp together, remote and full of secrets, yet men who were hard, reliable and plainly eager for action now it might be at hand.

Although as confident as he had been from the outset, Morell wasn't about to wager on success. The thing was, he had journeyed across this wilderness once before and knew he would have become lost a hundred times but for his Pawnee guide. He had faith in Longley as a trailsman. But whether you could actually trail a bunch of outlaws through a vast and overpowering landscape which left virtually no sign of man's passage on its ancient, iron-hard skin was something Morell would have to see happen before he started in spending the fat bonus he was promised should they achieve Vallance's twin goals at trail's end.

A flock of huge turkey buzzards circling lazily guided them to the shoot-out site. Leaving the party in the shade of a cliffside, Longley and Morell kicked on to reach the bleached, pear-shaped landmark boulder which seemed unremarkable by daylight in contrast with its ghostly appearance in the smoke-shrouded gloom and uncertainty of the gunfight.

They glimpsed the copse from a distance and rode on by to top out a bulging crest in an ancient range which Longley reckoned had to be the direction the nightriders had been fixing to take when overrun.

The ground beneath them here was rocky and tufted sparsely by grudging growths of ocotillo, paintbrush and the occasional clump of mesquite.

Joe got down and led the way on through the gap, eyes never leaving the earth, Morell mooching along behind. A dozen times he halted to examine what might have been a hoof-scrape or a plant damaged in transit by human passage.

Nothing.

After an hour of this Morell began fidgeting, rolled cigarettes, threw them away half-smoked, kept glancing at the sky where there wasn't a solitary cloud to mute the power of the August sun.

He was on the verge of calling a halt to the search when Longley finally spotted what he was looking for. Just a few yards ahead he glimpsed a lighter mark upon a rock, which on closer inspection proved to be a fresh hoof-scrape.

Hunkering down, he rubbed his fingers lightly over the mark then held them to his nostrils. He winked over his shoulder at Morell. Barely detectable was the faint metallic smell of the steel horseshoe that had left the sign.

'Pay dirt,' he grunted, rising to unbuckle his canteen from the pommel and gaze around. Until now he'd paid little attention to the changing terrain, for none of it would mean anything unless he got a line on the route Red Hatch had taken from the shoot-out site.

They were in a tight little draw where Spanish dagger spiked upwards from sloping walls. After slaking his thirst he swung astride and faced north. With the added height he could see over the rim to take in a mile-wide stone landscape of devil's marbles, and beyond this the tumbled mass of prehistoric stone, talus and soaring turrets of the range called Chickashay.

Beyond the Chickashay lay the real wilderness.

'That's the way he went,' he announced. 'Cut back and fetch them. I'll ride on up to the pass just to make double sure.'

Morell squinted at the heat haze shimmering off the range like smoke.

'What if you run into someone ugly?'

'I'll handle it.'

'Don't get too cocky just because you found a piece of sign.'

'I'll see you when you catch up.'

'Whatever you say, Field Marshal.'

Longley just grinned and rode off towards the range.

Chiller scratched his hairy belly through a tear in his shirt as he watched Swede working on the stallion's sore feet.

'How's he comin'?' he demanded.

'OK, I guess.'

'You guess? What's that supposed to mean? Is he gonna be still limping when we meet up with the money man, or not?'

'Depends on how long it takes Petrie to get here, I reckon.'

'You being flip with me, boy? If you're being flip, you could lose an ear. I hate flip guys. Flip guys are like–'

'I ain't being flip, damnit, Ned. I'm just tuckered and hot and need a bath in a tub of cold beer, is all.'

The murderous old badman with the missing teeth clapped hands to bent knees and roared laughing, his meanness gone in an instant, the echoes of his great braying whinny, so incongruous in such a setting, batting back and forth overhead and startling a drowsing owl into flight from a nearby Joshua tree.

'Ah, and you young bums wonder why I love this life,' Lucky Ned beamed, dabbing at his eyes . 'It's the goddamn pure fun of it, is what. Imagine setting out here all the way to hell with its trousers down, away from anything that even smells like civilization, nursing a danged hoss worth half a million and no way of knowing if we're going to come out of this whole thing rich, busted, jumping out of our skins or dead as George Washington – and this no-account owlhoot bum can still sass back and make a man laugh ... I do declare.'

Lucky Ned's laughter was usually infectious but it failed to work its magic on the others today.

Almost overnight the gang's great caper – beginning at a rich man's spread down Wigwam way and leading all the long miles north across the Krees to the Sawteeth before skirting Crow Creek to cross three wild valleys to finally reach their destination –had seemed to lurch and falter.

Chiller had been prepared to overlook the slaughter at the Slot of the two trail bums he'd hired to divert pursuit, despite the worrying fact that every indication showed the men had been killed by a pro who really knew his business.

But Crow Creek was where his real troubles had erupted when Hatch and Roth took a hammering, bringing home the realization they were being seriously pursued.

Yet he still could laugh and was still chuckling as he turned away from the stallion to catch Red Hatch watching him warily from the shade where the remuda dozed. Immediately his grin was replaced by a black scowl that could cower a man at twenty paces.

Maybe Hatch and Roth had done well to identify the slim-hipped boy dallying around town with a local chippy as Kid Cobain, he was prepared to concede. And had he been there himself he would have surely ordered the pair to take him out while they had the chance; he had no quarrel with that.

But they'd fouled up.

Instead of nailing the notorious gunslinger when they had the chance, all the pair had succeeded in doing was to rouse the whole damn place and bring the Kid's possemen pals roaring into Crow Creek like the US Cavalry.

The result was Sugar Lee dead and likely – they weren't sure of this yet – Vallance's posse provisioning up to follow them into the wilderness.

Lucky Ned had horse-whipped men for less, but in this heat it hardly seemed worthwhile. So he ignored a grey-faced Hatch and tramped on by the mouth of the cave shared by Stag Meager and Cripple Creek Lloyd to seek out lanky Gravedigger. He found him seated cross-legged on the rock apron of a smaller cave sucking an opium pipe and staring south-east.

Gravedigger was Chiller's top lieutenant and the man who had overseen the whole Champion deal with Boss Petrie. Opium relaxed him, so he claimed. He seemed plenty calm as he continued to focus on the south-west, the route their scout would return by after checking out the repercussions of the shoot-out at Oak Hill.

'Anything?' Chiller growled, knowing there wasn't. The other shook his head and the leader lowered his sixty-year-old rump to an ammunition case with a grunt and produced the makings.

This was high up upon the rearing escarpment of the Montonosas, the granitic bulwark which formed the northern wall of Twisted Valley, first and largest of the wilderness valleys when approaching from the south. The ancient Indian caves, abandoned so far back in time nobody knew if they'd been Apache, Navajo or some unknown other, were unique both in their size and complexity as well as the view they offered, an essential for badmen eternally on the run from one danger or another.

Unlike the fantastic stone worlds of spectacular desolation lying immediately to the north, Twisted Valley was two-thirds sand, and a man only had to squint his eyes on a day of brain-boiling heat like today to believe he was in Death Valley at the wrong end of the season.

Luckily the heat didn't affect Lucky Ned. Nor did cold, thirst, hard times, faithless women or men in saloons with names like Ed or Duke who dealt off the bottom of the deck. He'd weathered all such perils and worse over half a lifetime and planned on doing so for the next forty years or more. What did irk him was men who let him down. Like Hatch and Roth –or clients who couldn't keep to a schedule.

'What's the betting Petrie's got hisself lost up in the Whitefoot or Cripple Creek,' he grumbled when he had his smoke going to his satisfaction. 'Never met a rich man with a sense of direction as I recall.'

'He's only a day overdue, Ned.'

'Lot can happen in a day. Ask Sugar Lee.'

Gravedigger turned his head. He was a thirty-year-old badman with a fifty-year-old face – lined, seamed, ravaged and unutterably sad. No other name but the one he was tagged with would have fitted.

'What about Cobain? Hatch swears he's with the posse. Who hires a Cobain by the week? Almost nobody can even afford that little viper's fee to pistol down the bastard what's sleepin' with his wife.'

Lucky Ned's weathered features were bleak as he gazed out over the sandy wastes reaching away westward, rippling in the heat and seeming to drowse beneath the biggest sky his evil old eyes had ever seen.

'Vallance must be able to afford it, boy. OK, I know the scouts ain't actually seen Vallance yet, but we know it's gotta be him. The law down south gave up early – dead scared of catching us, I reckon. There's bounty on our heads and a big reward for the stud, but that wouldn't even cover the horse feed expenses of an outfit the size Red sighted in Crow Creek.' He nodded emphatically. 'It's Vallance, for sure. And if he can afford the Kid, who else might he have riding with him?'

Gravedigger digested this for some time, a long lean scarecrow of a man leaning back on bony elbows.

Then he asked, 'So, let's say it's the biggest and meanest posse ever, Ned? Something we never counted on. How do we handle it?'

Chiller was saved from replying straight by the sudden appearance of a speck of movement against the stone, way off south-east, brought them both to their feet.

The sand had not encroached where that distant horseman rode. Out there the scaly red ground descended gradually from the barricade of the hills into an ocean of bare red knolls, like waves, rolling away eastward. Black butts reared their flat heads along the tangent Fargo was taking, and soon they realized he was coming in fast.

The news was bad. Somehow they'd expected it would be. Fargo reported nine men on their trail cutting across country at speed for the notch through the Chickashay hills at this very moment. Fargo had got his binoculars on them but briefly, just long enough to identify a heavily-armed posse, well-mounted with spare saddlers and a supply wagon – an outfit as professional-looking as any as he'd ever seen dogging anybody.

By this the whole bunch was gathered round Lucky Ned, who, as always, proved a good man to have at the helm when the weather broke rough.

'Can that stud travel?' he barked at the tow-headed Swede. The man nodded and Chiller spat on the hot stone, squinted at the sky. 'Simple then. We planned to meet our client here, but seeing as he's running late, we'll cut north and meet him up-trail, mebbe around Three Hole Basin. We'll jest complete our business there, hand over the neddy, pocket our cash, then skee-daddle long afore any hard-nosed kind of posse can get within fifty miles. This is just a hiccup.

What counts is we've got the horse and Petrie's bringing the money. All right, what are we waiting for?'

Camp was broken within minutes. They planned to be well across the Montonosas and travelling Cripple Creek Canyon long before the posse got even halfway across the three valleys.

Lucky Ned had been careful about their sign before, now he grew obsessive. Meager led the way, selecting the flintiest ground that would leave least sign. Gravedigger rode drag armed with a mesquite branch, brushing away anything that might catch the eye of an expert tracker.

It was characteristic of Lucky Ned Chiller that he appeared vaguely unhappy – not nervous – as the miles flowed behind. He'd been born bad and fighting back, and throughout his brutal life fighting had become the very stuff of life to him, as a hundred scars would attest.

Sure, he was eager to finalize the biggest job he'd ever attempted. He only regretted not being able to achieve both that goal and get to annihilate that bloodhound outfit dogging their tracks.

The Kid liked his own company best.

Throughout the heat of the long afternoon the slender figure on the fat brown mare had trailed a mile and more behind the posse, ignoring the heat, dreaming his own sick dreams which were better than any others he'd ever heard of, occasionally halting Maybell to admire a basking rattler, a high buzzard or a scorpion on a rock – anything that killed.

Up ahead the rubes were getting excited about the way wonderman Longley seemed able to pick up repeatedly sign where there apparently wasn't any.

So the Farmer was good at his trade. So? A wolf or an average-to-good house hound could track fifty times better than any long-boned cow-pusher ever could. But tell him, where was the critter who could whip a gun out of leather and cut a playing card in half edge-on at fifty feet faster than a man could spit?

Longley was a clodhopper, Morell a has-been and Vallance just another stuffed shirt who thought he was something because he could afford to hire others to do what he didn't have the guts to do himself. As for the rest; he'd be five years dead before he got to be as dull and boring as the smartest of them. Which only left the horses, which he'd sooner pal up with than their riders, if he had his druthers.

The landscape drifted by and the mare sweated a freshet as the full power of the Burning Stone sun made its presence felt.

Languidly he built a smoke but didn't enjoy it. They were crossing a vast sandy valley along what the Farmer claimed to be their quarry's tracks. This was always the hard part of any job for the Kid. The riding and the waiting. His idea of a perfect job was when you walked into a saloon to meet your client, he pointed out some jasper over by the bar, you gunned him down, grabbed the money and heeled out of town like a skunk with its tail on fire.

In reality he'd actually had one job like that ideal, down in Juarez a year ago. All the others had involved delays, trailing, and putting up with rubes and hicks and stumblebums who thought they were something. Like Longley and Morell.

Seemed to him they were getting almost pally, that pair. Figured. Nobodies always needed buddies and steady women and all that kind of hoopla to boost them up and make them feel like they were something. But when you were the Kid, you really were something. You knew it, everyone else knew it, so every time you happened to be alone you were enjoying the best company in the world.

That thought sustained him over several miles until he suddenly realized it was growing dark and he could no longer see the riders up ahead.

Maybell started and broke instantly into a lope as heels banged horsehide. He covered a fast mile before topping out a plateau to see shielded campfires some distance ahead in the lee of a rocky overhang.

Weary men glanced up from their evening chores as he dusted in and bounced out of the saddle with the agility of a rodeo rider.

'All right!' he hollered, 'where's the oyster steak – and who said I didn't want branch water with my whiskey?'

This was his idea of being amusing. None shared his notion. The men were all hot, dirty, dry, hungry, saddle-stiff and grumpy. Some smiled faintly but only because you could never be sure how the Kid would take it if you didn't. Others just stared and Cobain stared right back, hoping someone might take offence, but of course they never did.

He strolled across to the covered wagon where Ike Clancy was setting up a camp stove on the tailgate to cook supper for

Vallance and Webb, who were up in the vehicle resting with only the soles of their boots visible.

Morell walked by with a vague nod and the Kid stared after him. He looked about sharply. Where was the wonder scout? Mostly since quitting Crow Creek, wherever you saw one you saw the other.

'All right,' he said to driver Clancy. 'Where's old corn-shucking Farmer Longley?'

Clancy set some touch paper to a little pile of kindling and flames shot up brightly. He nodded northward. 'Gone ahead some.'

'What the hell for? Even he can't read sign in the dark, can he? Or is that another one of his slippery tricks?'

'Said he's hoping to maybe catch a glimpse of a campfire or something like. Night-sign, he called it.'

'I know what I call it,' Cobain flared, riled in an instant. 'Grandstanding, is what.' He made an impatient gesture. 'He won't find beans and he knows it. Can't you see what makes that boring old ploughwalker feel he's more than just a boring old ploughwalker? It's all you nobodies sucking up and telling him what a fire-cracker trailsman he is, so he feels he's got to go off pull some stunt, or fake one, just to get all you bums bowing low and singing alleluia.'

A figure stirred up in the shadowed wagon and Vallance sat up looking beat and unshaven. He also looked peeved.

'What's all the commotion about?' he demanded querulously. 'What's bothering you, Kid?'

Cobain couldn't have explained even if he'd tried. Right from day one Longley had riled him, initially because of the way it seemed nobody was able to rile him.

But it was the incident at Crow Creek that had sown the seeds of genuine enmity. The Farmer had saved his life then galloped off and nailed one of his attackers. He couldn't get that one out of his craw, and now Longley was off searching for even more glory.

He was muttering curses when inspiration hit. The hell with sitting round waiting for wonderman to return. He was bored and chockful of energy, as was mostly the case, especially at night. Added to that, he knew what to look for on a manhunt just as well if not better than any hick.

'Hey, where you going, Kid?' Clancy called as he vaulted into the saddle and went storming away.

No reply came from the darkness.

# CHAPTER 9

## STONE GODS, IRON MEN

Longley rode alone.

Mostly he liked company when travelling the trails. But this was different. Tonight, for the first time in more than two years, he was riding the wilderness and that was an experience like no other, a feast for the spirit even if he was obliged to concentrate almost exclusively on the moonwashed landscape ahead as the dun carried him steadily into the north.

Nothing in Twisted Valley had changed. To his west lay the dunes rippling away as far as the eye could see, in the early night, to the east his first glimpses of the magnificent Burning Stone landmarks of buttes and crumbling towers, brooding rock fortresses and impossible pinnacles seeming to reach to the stars.

He reached out to pat the horse's neck and it tossed its head in response. Man and beast were part of the wilderness and the night was their companion.

He paid little attention to the rocky ground beneath them. The moonlight was brilliant, but night light was never strong enough for searching for faint sign. He was keeping sharp for something else, anything else that might hint which route across the distant Montonosas the quarry might take, if indeed Chiller was bent on striking even deeper north.

Glancing back he saw no sign of life.

By now they'd know he was gone and may not be coming back.

In all his experience in the wild he'd never done this before – quit on a client.

It had to happen.

Throughout the hunt he'd been alert to something disturbing about Vallance and his posse like an uneasy undercurrent, an ever-strengthening suspicion that the expedition had to be more than a simple hunt for a horse. He sensed it in averted glances, in the way conversations dried up when he approached. But his unease had become almost conviction during the showdown meeting with Vallance just hours earlier which he'd hoped might answer all his questions but only succeeded in raising more.

He'd killed a man as part of his job and might have to kill again. He could live with that. But now he needed some kind of proof that the job really was the kind a man should be prepared to kill or even die for. Of the entire bunch, from Vallance down to Clancy, he reckoned only Morell might have some genuine integrity, but doubted he could rely on that gunman to level fully with him either. So, directly following the parley with the big man he'd found himself deciding between just two choices: quit and head home, or admit he might be judging the whole set-up wrongly or too harshly, in which case he had a responsibility to go prove it out one way or another.

He was leaving clear sign to ensure the posse could follow him even by night. But he would continue on alone until he felt he understood the set-up completely then make his choice. He could either quit, or eat humble pie and link up with them again to see the thing through, as originally agreed.

Weighty matters. Yet it was good to escape the camp. A real scout often required solitude. Company and conversation could distract a man just as readily out here as in a crowded town.

The horse tossed its head as an owl suddenly flew by with the rush of heavy wingbeats.

He followed the bird with his eyes, and when he looked ahead again, he saw it. Halfway up the steep face of the Montonosa Hills, all moonlight and shadow, a momentary speck of light had flickered once and was gone.

He reined in, reached for his field glasses. He used them expertly to bring the hills in close. He pinpointed the area where the light had shown, but it was not repeated. As he played the glasses to and fro he realized that the dark blobs he was focusing upon on a high ledge were a feature named The Caves of the Ancient Ones, where he'd camped on more than one occasion.

He lowered the glasses slowly to his chest, his expression intent and focused as his mind raced. Someone was up there, or had been a short spell back. What interested him was whether it might be outlaws or just some innocent desert drifter. He wanted to believe it might be Chiller, although he calculated they should be well across the Montonosas by now if they still were striking due north.

He glanced over his shoulder once more, features tight with concentration. Discipline and long habit suggested he ride back and report his finding to Vallance. But instinct and a scout's innate senses warned him that whoever was up there could be across the hills and lost forever in Creation Valley by the time he and the full party could reach the caves.

Intuition won out.

Jumping down, Longley grabbed up some loose white stones to fashion an arrow-shaped emblem in the middle of the trail pointing directly towards the hills. He collected more stones to stuff into his saddlebags then fished around for a pencil stub, ripped a page from his trailbook and scrawled a hasty note:

Morell
Somebody at caves halfway up hills.
Checking it out. Follow stones.

The dun grunted as he filled leather and kicked on. The scenery grew increasingly weird and spectacular as he put the quick miles behind him. He barely noticed. Longley the lover of lonely places had been replaced by Longley the hard-nosed trail scout. He rarely took his eyes from the Montonosas which failed to show any further sign of life.

The moon was climbing high by the time he was working his way up through the foothills. He took to halting every fifty yards or so as he climbed, using intense listening. Timber blotted out the caves from his sight and night critters rustled in the brush. The higher he climbed the quieter he moved, until the horse kicked a stone.

He was making too much noise.

Offsaddling he led his mount into a tamarack grove and tied it up. 'Just take it easy... I'll be back.' There was no point in anyone telling Joe Longley horses couldn't understand plain English. He knew better. The dun was one smart animal.

Rifle in hand and choosing his footing with care, he continued to ease his way up through boulders and thinning trees until he was eventually catching glimpses of the light-hued ridge line and the dark-mouthed caves beyond.

Still no sight or sound of life. Had that smoker – he was sure that what he'd glimpsed had been a man lighting up – quit and taken cover? Or maybe he was supported by gun-toting buddies all lying low just waiting for him to shove his head up above the firing line?

Why don't you try and scare yourself, Longley? he asked himself, then immediately dropped to ground, falling atop the Winchester.

Somewhere, maybe as close as fifty yards away, a man had cleared his throat.

He waited five minutes before rising. In total silence he threaded his way through what remained of the trees before angling off to the right to avoid coming up directly in front of the caves.

Eventually he came to a halt pressed up against the natural broad ledge which formed the long stone apron before the dwellings of the Ancient Ones.

Reaching down his fingers closed over a small pebble. Rising, he flicked it high to land on the far side of the caves. It came down with a clatter. There was a curse, and next moment the silhouette of a man appeared from a cave mouth holding a revolver.

Joe rested his rifle upon the rock apron and hissed, 'Freeze! I've got you cold!'

Pivoting, the silhouette whirled and fired. For the shaved tip of a second Longley held his fire, thinking of that dead man back at Oak Hill. When a second bullet whipped by he squinted along the barrel and squeezed trigger.

Nobody could miss at that range.

By the time the gun echoes were muttering away into silence, Longley was up on the apron approaching the crumpled figure which hadn't moved.

Grim jawed, he kicked the revolver away and saw blood soaking the back of the man's vest where his .32 slug had gone clean through.

There was no need to turn him over.

He felt cold and detached as he conducted the perfunctory search. Plainly a bunch of men had camped here for maybe a day or two. There was litter, dead fires, empty bottles, horse sign. Nothing to say who they were, which meant he had no option but to check the dead man out after all.

He rolled him over with his toe. He was as loose and limp as something that had never been alive. The face staring up at him was gaunt, beard-stubbled, sunburnt and mean as snake juice. His garb showed evidence of a rough life spent in the open but the oiled gunbelt was of high quality.

A lookout left behind to keep watch in case of pursuit, was his best guess. Too bad he hadn't been up to the task.

Going through the pockets he found the usual tobacco, coins and notes, various odds and ends along with a yellowed newspaper clipping. He straightened as he unfolded the paper and scanned it by the slowly strengthening daylight. It was a brief report of a bank hold-up in Utah in which three people had died, a crime attributed to the 'notorious Chiller gang'.

The following minutes saw him scouring the area beyond the end of the ledge on the western side, where a man with half an eye could have deciphered that a party of five or six men had ridden away leading several horses. When he had followed the clear sign a mile he came to an animal track leading northward directly over the Montonosas.

Heading downslope to collect his horse he briefly considered striking back the way he'd come and then keep going, back through Crow Creek, down the windy flanks of eastern Kree Plains and all the long miles beyond without stopping until he raised the rooftops of the Tadpole.

Just wishful thinking.

By the time he was feeding the dun red corn nubbins from his pack he knew the only direction he would or could travel now, was north.

Scout's code; you never quit mid-job even if you mistrusted the men you worked for, had to kill to keep going.

Simply, what he would do was trail that bunch before it got clear away then lie low and wait for the posse to catch up.

Only then might he quit.

The Kid giggled in the cool of the night.

The abrupt stutter of gunfire from somewhere north had sounded so startling in the hushed morning hour, that a man just had to laugh.

He found the gunshots exciting, thrilling.

It told him that while respectable folk and so-called tough possemen snored in their blankets, out here in the ass-end of nowhere, where you normally might expect to hear nothing more menacing than the bark of a coyote or the whip-de-woo of a whistler bird, there was danger afoot and bad company abroad, with maybe even something genuinely big and scary brewing.

He was ready to wager the new striped pink shirt he'd bought back at the town that old sobersides Longley was mixed up in this somewhere.

His good humour vanished.

He knew now just how smart he'd been to dog the Farmer's trail. That one might be just a dumb hick ploughman but he sure knew the scouting business. He now figured Longley had struck trouble out there across the valley – nothing would convince him otherwise. It added up that it had to have something to do with the horsethieves, and if things were finally rushing towards some kind of climax then his place was out there, not here.

Kid Cobain had a lot of pride to recover.

He raked with spur and Maybell broke into a wheezing run. He made a bee-line for the region of the Montonosas where the shots had sounded. In so doing he missed Longley's stone direction arrow and note left upon the high slope.

These weren't discovered for another hour when Morell led the posse down off Oak Hill. He retrieved the note, scanned it and passed it up to Vallance perched high on the wagon's spring seat. The big man scowled as he read then screwed it into a tight little ball and flung it aside.

'They're making more money than they ever will again in their lives, yet they don't have the slightest notion of the responsibility that goes with any high-paying assignment!' he said savagely. He whirled on Clancy the driver with a vicious curse. 'Well, what are you gawping at? You heard what Longley said. "Due north up the hills." Get this benighted box of bolts moving, damn you. The rest of you – ho!'

Hard-faced riders didn't seem to notice how the brilliant moonlight briefly illuminated the length and breadth of Twisted Valley, which took on the beauty of a serum calendar illustration aglow with shades of purple, gold, vermilion and gentle hues of green as the party surged off down the slope.

An unusually grim Morell was first to reach the valley floor. He felt Longley had let him down, while a persistent inner voice asked if maybe it wasn't the other way around.

All eyes were focused on the steep trail winding down through the gaunt grey stones flanking the faint Indian trail leading into Three Holes Canyon from Krakia Plateau.

'Reckon it's them?'

The Swede looked hopeful but stood behind an unsaddled horse at the remuda with his Colt angled across the animal's back, just in case.

'Of course it is, you fool!'

Lucky Ned sounded more confident than he felt. The way the chips had been falling over the past forty-eight hours, it could well prove to be a squadron of US Cavalry under the command of a full Brevet-Colonel approaching from above. First Roth killed; now Mawby overdue in from the caves. On the positive side, this section of Three Holes Canyon lay squarely on the southern route Petrie was supposed to be following. But he was already way overdue; it could be anybody coming down off the plateau.

'Yeehahhh!'

Every outlaw in Three Holes Canyon but one jerked his head around at that sudden startling shout. What they saw was rugged Fargo perched atop the wagon waving his hat and grinning like a fool.

'Jest caught a glimpse of them, Ned,' the man beamed. 'Ugliest little runt I ever seen perched atop what looks like a thoroughbred Arab. That sounds like your party, don't it?'

Lucky Ned ceased scowling and toying with his gun handles as the Utah party suddenly swung into clear view below the plateau, laughing, shouting and waving their hats.

'Hey there, Ned, you old rogue. Knew you'd make it. You got my nag?'

Standing with boots wide-planted and hands on beefy hips, the outlaw boss just nodded his cruddy old felt hat and shot an eloquent glance across at Swede. The towhead nodded proudly. This had been the gang's most daring and high-paying job ever. When first approached by Petrie through a contact with the proposition of travelling hundreds of miles from Utah down to Stud Ranch, and stealing the most famous blood horse in the south-west, Chiller had been beset by doubts. At first. Then the sheer bald-faced nerve of the proposal began to appeal to him, until within a mere matter of days he found himself leading his men south, full of whiskey, optimism and plans for luxurious retirement upon completion of the impossible mission.

It was all an eager Boss Petrie could do to shake hands and say howdy before looking around for sign of the stallion.

Sensing the Utahan's urgency, the Swede wasted no time. He was grinning hugely as he appeared around a rock shoulder leading a horse, the sight of which brought instant tears to Boss Petrie's tiny rat eyes.

Champion Minaret Star Song – so the stallion's pedigree read. Petrie knew its lineage backwards. Originally imported from Ireland it had built an instant reputation in the Eastern states before Robert Vallance hocked his soul to the bank to purchase the stallion and have it shipped to Stud Ranch down in the Wigwam country.

That had been then. Now with his progeny dazzling fine horse-lovers in a dozen states and territories, this was the champion of champions and looked it every inch despite the hardships of the trek northward.

A blind man could have seen this horse's quality. Classic head, a long and graceful neck, deep-chested and thick through the heart with short withers sloping into a strong back and slender legs capable of propelling the characteristically powerful hindquarters common to the breed, which guaranteed that virtually any of Champion's progeny destined for the racetrack invariably did brilliantly.

But maybe what runty, squinty, 'horse-lover' Boss Petrie liked best about his new acquisition was that it was – or had been – the property of Robert Wilson Vallance.

When Petrie and Chiller clapped one another on the back and executed a little jig of triumph it was the signal for both groups to get together and loosen up some. It had been a long and testing journey south from his Utah spread for the Petrie party, an even longer and damned dangerous one for the rustling gang. Rambunctious Lucky Ned might have proposed a real blow-out to mark the occasion had he been less concerned by the fact that one of his men was overdue.

He'd posted Mawby back at the caves where they'd camped to keep watch over the valley for a time hours before rejoining them here. The man was yet to show, so Chiller detached himself from the group and looked about for Donny Longtime, the Paiute trailsman who'd been with the bunch a long time. But the Paiute was noplace to be found.

'Where the hell is he?' Chiller demanded in sudden alarm, big hairy head swivelling this way and that. 'Anyone seen my no-account redskin? What's going on here? First Mawby overdue, now that scalp-hunter–'

'It's OK, Ned,' a black-bearded desperado cut in. He gestured. 'He went slinking off back into them rocks yonder by the pools a spell back. Told me this is a spooky place and he meant to go check it out. You know? Like he checks everything, him being part Paiute and part dog-wolf.'

Chiller's scowl played over the three rock pools or *tinajas* that gave the basin its name then swept upwards over the bulging face of the cliff rearing above the most reliable water supply in the whole valley.

'Danged heathen savage...' he muttered. Then he remembered it was his big pay day at last and swung on his heels to go remind Boss Petrie of that fact.

They rode in single file at a brisk pace darkly silhouetted against the bloated summer moon that hung massively in the southern sky over the Vermilion Cliff. Vallance's posse less two. The rancher, Webb, Clinton, Santone, Dalton, Flagg and Morell.

No Longley and no Kid.

Morell cut his steely gaze back over the line and dropped a curse that was engulfed by drumming hoofbeats. The tip of Longley's terse note fluttered from the breast pocket of his fringed buckskin jacket. He was mad as hell at his scout, but at least they had a notion where he was and what he was doing.

The Kid could be out here someplace either ahead or behind them for some weird reason of his own. Or asleep in a whorehouse back in Crow Creek for all anybody knew.

He'd known that fast-gun hellion would prove one huge headache out here, while at the same time admitting they'd really needed someone of his calibre along.

But what the hell value was a hot-shot scout and a six-shooter wizard if they quit on you just when the chips were down?

He turned back to the way ahead.

They were clattering through a forest of monumental stone formations which loomed on either side, shaped, moulded and twisted into fantastic shapes that resembled nameless monolithic gods.

The Montonosa Hills began to loom closer above the titanic stone columns and Morell glimpsed yet another scatter of the small, white pebbles Longley was dropping from time to time to show them the route.

His jaw muscles worked. Somehow he'd come grudgingly to build up a high regard for their scout on the long trail. Yet he'd never expected to find himself totally relying on the man's skills and character to lead them to the horse and whoever they might find with it when they got there.

## CHAPTER 10

### GUNMEN'S CANYON

Longley lay sprawled belly-flat on the black rock shelf high above the rock pan pools where, directly below, some dozen men with wide hats and tied-down guns were talking animatedly and circling about on the broad rock apron like guests at a hardcase hoedown.

Approaching Three Holes Basin by the south track earlier he knew he'd struck pay dirt the moment he sighted fireglow through the trees ahead and picked up the murmur of voices.

Having camped at the basin several times in the past he knew exactly what he had to do: stash his horse and tackle the steep climb across the loose shale slopes to access the cliff that reared steep and sheer directly above the *tinajas*.

Minutes later, silent and unsuspected, he was staring down upon the unmistakable bulk of Lucky Ned Chiller, a face and physique made familiar by a thousand Wanted dodgers, welcoming a party of wilderness travellers coming down off Krakia Plateau. Longley heard the by-now familiar name of 'Petrie' drifting up to him as a runty little man with the strut of a bantam cock greeted and was being greeted by everyone else like all were blood brothers, until interrupted by the sudden dramatic appearance of the stallion.

Champion was still the focus of attention, both theirs and his. Longley was elated, if only briefly, for he'd successfully tracked the rustlers down at the end of a hundred-mile hunt, and the great horse was plainly unharmed. But there was already a hint of guilt to take the edge off his triumph, for the scene unfolding before his gaze was proving virtually exactly as Vallance had predicted. Here was Lucky Ned amiably handing the horse he'd stolen over to Vallance's mortal enemy. What else had he expected?

So much for his hunches and suspicions of some secret and sinister Vallance agenda. The man had simply been hunting his stolen horse – just as any man would do. Of course, what he was witnessing here was a major crime in the making ... and he'd better figure out what he intended to do about it real fast. But it was tough to admit he could have been so wrong about Vallance's motives in mounting his deadly, high-priced posse, and wondered if this could be a sign that this trail scout had taken on one job too many, that he'd lost his old edge.

It had been instinctive for him to tally the numbers milling around down there, yet suddenly some sixth sense prompted him to count again, and the total came up one man short.

He stiffened.

Where had the man gone? And which one was missing?

He concentrated fiercely, for if there was one of them unaccounted for it could pose a danger to him. Face after unfamiliar face passed beneath his close scrutiny. He remembered the one in the charro pants, the guntoter with yard-wide shoulders. He remembered each man in turn but was still struggling to picture the missing one, whether he be outlaw or Petrie hand, when his trained scout's memory belatedly clicked into gear.

The Indian!

A sorrel-skinned Paiute had been prominently at Chiller's side shortly before the Petrie party came down off the plateau, but was now nowhere to be seen.

His double-check only confirmed his suspicion. There was definitely no Indian down there now and he sensed there hadn't been in some time.

He was about to shoot a wary glance over his shoulder when he froze, feeling his neck hair lift. From the corner of his eye, down below by the central rock pan, he'd detected stealthy movement. The Indian! said his mind. He focused intently. There it was again. He glimpsed a hat crown and a section of shirtsleeve protruding from behind a bulky canting boulder. But surely Chiller's Paiute had been garbed in greasy black leathers head to toe? Whoever was lurking behind that chunk of stone had to be a real flashy dude ... and didn't that showy shirt look familiar?

What happened next, he recalled later, was like watching a magic lantern show where there was a defect in the mechanism and figures and objects seemed to move realistically enough yet in slowed-down motion.

Firelight winked on the gun barrel which suddenly sprouted into view beyond the rock shoulder. In the same instant the head and shoulders of Kid Cobain reared up and a billowing cloud of gunsmoke spewed from his weapon as the gun exploded to engulf the basin in shock waves of sound.

Directly across the rocky floor where figures were clustered about the great horse, the man he'd identified as Boss Petrie cried out in agony and was falling sideways when the now hidden .44 Smith & Wesson churned for a second time.

It didn't miss, and Longley heard someone holler, 'Boss has been kilt!' as he leapt to his feet.

He didn't know if he cursed in protest as he stared down in horror. The runty little man hadn't moved. He certainly appeared dead. Gunned down in cold blood by the Kid. On Vallance's orders? What else could it be?

His mind was racing like a trip hammer as the noise of wild shouting punctuated by yet another harsh shot came surging up from below to be trapped, echoing and ugly beneath his overhanging rock roof. Yet he still heard the sharp clang of steel striking rock where he'd lain just seconds before.

He saw the knife bounce away and whirled as the lithe Indian launched himself at him like a striking panther, teeth locked in a silent snarl as he whipped a second blade from his belt.

Longley's rifle was in his hand but there was no time to use it. He let it fall, then barely had time to drop his shoulder into the gut as the Paiute struck. The man was small but seemed to be fashioned from wang and rawhide. The shoulder charge belted the breath out of the scrawny body and the stink of bad teeth and foul foodstuff gushed over Longley's face as he desperately parried the knife blow with his elbow.

Steel bit his flesh.

He ducked his head to one side as the red blade fanged out for his throat. He raised his aim to block out a second lightning thrust. Blood poured from his shoulder yet he felt nothing. He was fighting for his life and the smoky, greasy smell of the buck engulfed him as he swayed back for balance then pistoned a right fist hard into the heart.

The man coughed in agony but still didn't speak. It was like being locked in a fight to the death with an animal. Longley felt the knife point slice up his shirtsleeve. He backed up, sideslipped on smooth stone and went down on one knee. He heard the Paiute's hiss of triumph as he lunged in for the death blow. But Longley expected it and was ready. At the last split second, with the wicked blade hissing for his throat, he dropped low, seized two skinny legs in an iron grip and surged erect with the man twisting violently overhead, fighting to get free.

A scrabbling hand found his face. He bit into it with all his strength. The Indian howled and Joe felt the twisting body slacken in his grip for a moment. He pivoted and bent double. Swung like a sack, the Indian was smashed into a sharp-edged boulder with sickening force. Bone broke and blood was spilling from the contorted mouth as Longley used all his power to swing his man about him in a huge circle, once, twice, then released his two-handed grip.

The Indian flew far out into space and screamed all the way down to the basin floor.

Longley staggered and stood swaying in the rock shadow, breath tearing in his lungs and the sweat stinging his eyes almost blinding him. He sleeved his face and stared dully at the blood gushing from his shoulder. Dimly he made out figures beginning to clamber towards him. Beyond them was a shadowy swirl of men and horses locked in mortal combat, figures briefly illuminated by gunflashes in the confusion, still bodies sprawled on dark stone.

He'd guessed it had to be the posse, a thought confirmed when a shaft of light fell upon Santone on horseback pumping red stabs of boreflame at the enemy with both hands.

His course was suddenly crystal-clear. For a long time he'd battled against the growing conviction that his dollar-driven decision to scout for Vallance had been wrong. But he'd kept doggedly at it, had been forced to kill two men along the way before realizing in an instant that he'd signed on with the wrong man at the wrong time for all the wrong reasons.

He'd realized this late, but hopefully not too late. He rubbed his face and gathered up the rifle. Had to get away. Find the horse. Ride like hell. Had to...

He went plunging and stumbling across the ancient rock slide on legs made of rubber. A rifle crashed and lead whistled venomously close. He cannoned into a stone spur in deep shadow, reeled backwards. But his strength was returning and his head seemed clearer as he fixed the dun's position in his mind and started downward again.

Until belatedly realizing that although the basin was rocking to gunfire now no bullets were howling around him.

He reached a vantage point to peer down.

He sagged as he found himself staring into scene straight out of hell.

During his fight to the death with the Paiute, the posse had come sweeping into the rock pans clearing. Plainly Morell and Vallance had done an all-too-good job of following the trail he marked for them. He'd hoped to get in to the water holes, check whatever was taking place there then report back.

Too late for that now; too many dead men too late.

He blinked as a bar of smoky moonlight fell on the unmistakable figures of Vallance with two-gun Santone at his side trading fierce fire with shadows which leapt from boulder to boulder like demon dancers.

The two men seemed crazed to kill, their reckless frenzy confirming his understanding that the posse had been on a murder mission from the outset, recovery of the great horse incidental.

After all those miles on the trail, fate had conspired to bring all the elements of the Champion affair together in the same fateful hour: Petrie, Chiller, the great horse, Vallance's gunman posse and the Kid – with Joe Longley thrown in as a dazed witness to it all.

And both rich men were equally to blame. Petrie had committed a criminal act in inciting Chiller to steal the stallion, Vallance had hocked his soul to the money-lenders in order to finance the deadliest posse money could buy.

He leaned there like an old man.

Now at least one of the protagonists was dead and the misguided men who'd followed them were fighting it out like wild beasts who treasured nothing but their hatred.

He turned away.

He was all through here. He was heading back to Tadpole, if he could just survive Three Holes Basin. How far down the slope was he now...? Maybe it was time to cut left ... yes, there was the lightning-split tree and the cleft leading down to the hollow where he'd stashed the dun ... the man leaning against one of the dead branches, arms folded and grinning like a fool...

What man?

Joe blinked and lurched to a halt, the rifle a ton weight in his hand.

'Here he is, the wonder trailsman and badman-killer shows up at last. You're tardy, Farmer, right tardy. I've been nipping across to blast the odd Chiller scum, then cutting back here where you parked your horse, fearful I might miss you when you came back for it. Hey, now I come to notice, you're looking kind of poorly on it. You been in trouble, old ploughwalker?'

'Get the hell out of my way, Cobain! I saw you cut Petrie down like a dog, I know you started all this. But you were tagged for that dirty job right from the jump, weren't you? Kill Petrie. That's what the posse was all about... I know it now. The big money suckering me in to show you the way...'

Longley broke off.

The Kid had pushed himself off the limb and stood facing him squarely across thirty feet. He wasn't grinning now.

'You made me look a fool back at the town, Longley – and you loved it. You think you're something special but you're just a goddamn psalm-singin' Judas and I smelt it in you from day one. Well, you can make your play with that big old hillbilly gun any time you like, Farmer. This is the Kid's night to clean up all around, so let's get it over with. You're the next on my list, ploughwalker, even if you sure as hell won't be the last.'

Longley knew he was finished. He was alone and death stood before him. Yet he had no fear because he had the strength a man gets from knowing he'd always respected the good and fought against the bad.

Counting his life in seconds, he realized this had been destined to come from the moment he signed on for Vallance's gold, and now it was also curiously crystal-clear that when it did come it would be in the form of the Kid. He'd seen death in the man's eyes the first moment they met. No good crying foul now.

And found himself oddly wondering how the woman would survive when he didn't come back.

'So long, Marita,' he breathed, and jerked up his Winchester .32.

The clearing rocked to gunblasts and he saw a Smith & Wesson six-shooter spinning through the air in a glittering arc. He heard bullets slam living flesh yet felt no pain. But surely there was something amiss with his vision, for he seemed to be seeing the Kid staggering towards him, one gun gone and the other angled at the ground, moving stiffly like a boy up on stilts with eyes hideously wide as the small crimson stain on his shirtfront instantly spread to engulf his entire upper body in a hot red as he curved slowly forward and smashed into the earth with his face.

Joe dashed at his eyes and stepped back from the corpse as the figure holding the smoking gun came up from the draw.

'It's all in the timing,' drawled Morell. 'At least that's what Bill Hickok told me once. You OK, Farmer?'

He was too spent to be astonished. But he still needed to know. 'You killed him and saved my life!' His voice was ragged, almost querulous. 'So, what's the name of your game, Morell? Or is this a new one? You know? Like the game you all played to sucker me into all this in the first place.'

Morell glanced in the direction of the rock pans where the guns still raged. He was wounded. He didn't seem to care.

'We mightn't have much time, so I'll make it quick, Joe. Sure, I knew the job was to kill Petrie; I signed on for it. But somehow along the trail I got to studying myself and thinking plenty. Guess I saw what a better life you had than me, and soon I was starting to question everything. Anyway, tonight when it came time to really earn my pay I galloped in here to see the Kid going insane and butchering men like hogs – and suddenly knew I was past it...'

He paused a moment as gunfire surged and snarled from around the *tinajas*. His head shook with sudden massive weariness. He was limping as he came around the corpse.

'None of this here has anything to do with us, trail scout. They're mad and we're sane. At least that's how I figured it when I just pulled out – just like that. But I reckoned that wherever you were you might use a friend, so I just kept hid and kept tabs on the Kid, somehow guessing he might lead me to you, and so he did. So, feel up to riding?'

It was too much for Longley to take in all at once. 'You're quitting it? Everything?'

'Seems as good a time as any.'

'We ... we just quit?'

'That's what you were doing before Cobain jumped you ... wasn't it?' Morell nodded emphatically. 'You bet it was.' He swung away, glancing back over his shoulder. 'Coming? It's better riding tandem than one-out on a night like this.'

Longley was astonished at just how easy it was simply to walk away.

The summer was dying as two men rode south across the Kree Plains. They'd left chaos behind for others to clean up and try to make sense of, any which way they might. It wasn't their concern any longer. The south was calling – a man could scent it on these Kree winds which never ceased to blow.

In the distance dark bovine shapes emerged from the dust, shoulders hunched, huge horns swinging low.

Morell spoke, then winced a little as his horse missed its step, jarring his arm which had taken a flesh wound back at the basin.

He cursed softly and Longley glanced his way. 'You say something?'

'Rogue bulls.' He gestured at the distant cattle with his good arm. 'Live to fight, fight to live. You could catch them and gentle them ten years, yet the day you let them loose they'd start right back fighting again because it's in their blood and they can never change.'

'That meant to mean something?'

'Vallance and Petrie. Climbed to the top, fat and rich, but still just a pair of old range bulls inside. No mystery to it all. Simple as the sunset.'

'Who cares?' Longley meant it. He was no longer interested in explanations or understanding. Just riding.

'So? Where we heading, Joe?' He scowled.

'I'm going home.'

'To stay this time, I reckon?'

'You could be right.'

Joe leaned forward a little in his saddle, his posture unconsciously revealing his eagerness to cover the next mile, cross the next dry creek bed. Watching him, Morell's pale eyes held a glint of envy.

'Guess it feels good to have something to go back to, huh?' he said.

'Well, don't tell me you haven't. More

contracts, that sort of stuff?'

'Could be.' Morell's gaze was fixed on dusty distances. A silence, then: 'But I won't be taking any of them up.'

'How come?'

Instead of answering directly, Morell massaged his square jaw and frowned thoughtfully.

'You reckon we're a bit alike, Joe?'

Surprised, Longley considered a moment. 'Mebbe. I know we think alike on the trails. And the Kid reckoned we were a lot alike ... old stodgy Farmer and Lonely, the man without a friend...'

'That butcher had me fitted right. Thirty-eight next birthday and nobody to be with but the next chippy I take up with. I got to admit that right now I wouldn't mind standing in your boots. You know, piece of land, neighbours, something that belongs to you waiting...'

'And more work not done than any man could handle even if a day was forty-eight hours long.'

Longley suddenly laughed at himself. Of a sudden he was feeling good. Already the manhunt was fading in his mind. There would never be another for him. He'd wanted money, had worked for it, gotten most of it. But it hadn't been worth it except for the lesson he'd learned that you paid for whatever you got in this life. Before signing on with Vallance he'd forgotten the danger and killing of other jobs. Never again. He meant to live up to that name Cobain had hung on him – Farmer.

'So, what are you angling at?' he heard himself ask after a silence. 'You want to stay on at Tadpole while you mend. Is that it?'

Morell's hard, handsome face brightened. 'Now that's a notion,' he said, acting surprised. 'You sure? Hey...' He broke off with a frown. 'Sure, I'd admire to take up that offer, but I'm forgetting something. It's not just up to you, is it?'

Joe sobered. 'I make the decisions on my land.'

'As I recall, things were kind of uneasy with you and Marita before we pulled out. Couldn't help but notice you two hardly seemed to trade a dozen words.'

'She was sore. She was smarter than I was.'

'You expect her to be there?'

Joe just shrugged. But Morell wasn't to be put off. He was genuinely curious. 'Big job of work, looking after a place for weeks on end for a woman, even one as strong and loaded with character as Marita.'

'That how you see her?'

'That's how she is.'

'Yeah, you could be right.'

'Well, I'm still waiting for an answer. Will she be there or not?'

It seemed a long time before Longley gave a small smile and shook out the horse's bridle. 'Maybe,' he murmured. 'Let's go find out.'

The publishers hope that this book has given you enjoyable reading. Large Print Books are especially designed to be as easy to see and hold as possible. If you wish a complete list of our books please ask at your local library or write directly to:

**Dales Large Print Books**
Magna House, Long Preston,
Skipton, North Yorkshire.
BD23 4ND

This Large Print Book, for people
who cannot read normal print,
is published under the auspices of

## THE ULVERSCROFT FOUNDATION